Romance

Marian J. ... Memorial Library

W9-CAJ-540

3 2075 00185 6230

LOVE IN B MINOR

A Broken Dreams Novel

Come talk to me in my Facebook Group, Elodie's Cozy Nook (exclusive excerpts, giveaways, group discussion and more...)

Do you want to be entered in a **giveaway** every month? Sign up for my newsletter

Elodie Nowodazkij

LOVE IN B MINOR Copyright © 2016 by Elodie
Nowodazkij

All rights reserved. Printed in the United States of America.
No part of this book may be used or reproduced in any manner
whatsoever without written permission except in the case of brief
quotations embodied in critical articles or reviews.

This book is a work of fiction. Names, characters, businesses,
organizations, places, events and incidents either are the product of
the author's imagination or are used fictitiously. Any resemblance
to actual persons, living or dead, events, or locales is entirely
coincidental.

For information, contact elodie@elodienowodazkij.com or visit:
www.elodienowodazkij.com
Book and Cover design by Elodie Nowodazkij
First Edition: March 2016

Contents

Pour toi, Paris.

For you, Paris.

CHAPTER 1 – JEN

Kneeing a guy in the balls might not be the best idea.

And not because the guy in question is one of those up and coming actors everyone says will be the next Leonardo DiCaprio, but because I don't want my friend Alisha to get in trouble. This club is new in Paris, but is already considered to be the "it" club. It's full of important people, and Alisha begged her cousin every single day for the past three weeks to find a way to get us in. He's DJ-ing and his music is the only part of this evening that doesn't suck.

"I think Scorsese is going to ask me to play the main role in his next movie. He needs a hero who speaks French. Hello? I'm French." His voice is way too close to my ear and I scoot away. But he doesn't get it. "I've got to ask for my friend over there." He points to someone who could be a doppelganger of Justin Bieber. "Do you have another friend or a sister maybe? He's feeling lonely."

My heart tightens and my eyes lock on the bottles lined up behind the bar. But concentrating on their bright colors or on the way the bartender manages to pour four drinks at once doesn't stop the pain from nesting itself deep in my chest.

I *had* a sister.

"Did I say something wrong?" It seems Bjorn the Actor can be perceptive after all.

I inhale and exhale slowly.

If I lose it, it's going to be the second time this week. I couldn't hold back the tears after my ballet company's director—Igor—yelled at me telling me I should have stayed in New York. Those words resonated in my heart and as soon as I got to my apartment, I plopped myself on my couch, held one of the last drawings my sister did for me and let the tears fall.

Future DiCaprio leans in and his cologne's too strong, making me want to gag. "You need to cheer up, angel. Can I get you another drink?"

I shake my head, still staring straight ahead, hoping he finally gets the message.

"Come on, beautiful. I've heard some amazing things about American girls." Even his voice is sleazy.

I push his hand away from my shoulder. I really don't want to know what he's heard about American girls. Or about Asian girls. Or about black girls. Which I'm sure is going to come next, since he's already asked me where my parents were from. He probably wouldn't care that my great-grandparents on my mother's side came from Japan, and that my grandfather on my father's side was born in Guinea and played soccer in Ireland, where he met my grandmother. Their relationship was scandalous at the time. Both my parents were born in the US, and when I told him that, he snickered.

Asshole.

His French accent isn't even redeeming his assholery.

I stand up so fast the barstool almost falls, but I catch it and put on my leather jacket over my silky red halter top, leaving my barely sipped mojito on the counter. One of the perks of being nineteen in Paris. No need for fake ID. Even though tipping isn't as common here, I leave two euros next to my drink and the bartender nods my way with a smile that doesn't only say thank you, but also that she knows how annoying this guy is.

"I need some fresh air." My fake smile must resemble a grimace because he raises an eyebrow, looking confused, but I don't give him any time to reply. Instead, I shuffle through the bodies crowding the center of the VIP room.

Alisha is sitting in one of the corner booths. Laughing and leaning into Steve, who she met tonight. He's from Ohio and is apparently the new member of a rock band which is looking to make a comeback after some internal issues. Whatever that means. He's built like a footballer and is entirely bald—not Alisha's usual style, but she seems like she's having the time of her life.

"I'm going to get some fresh air," I whisper in her ear and she jumps up, shrieking so loudly heads turn our way. Even Bjorn the Actor. Crap.

"I didn't see you coming!"

"You did indeed look quite busy there." I smile at Steve, who grins back, showing one dimple. If his band makes it to the top, Alisha's going to have to deal with a bunch of groupies. She's usually a boyfriend type. Her last relationship lasted eighteen months and it's the first time she's been out since it ended. "I'll be back, I swear. I only need to escape Douchey McDouchey."

She frowns and glances at the bar, where Bjorn sits. He's looking for someone and I sure don't want to be found. "You can sit with us." She taps the seat next to her, but she and Steve seem way too cozy for me to impose.

"No. I'll be fine. The girl sitting behind us has been shooting me death glares ever since he bought me a drink. I'm pretty sure she's about to make her move, and I'm pretty sure he's not going to refuse."

"You're going to be cold." She eyes my opened jacket, which is more a fashion statement than anything else. I checked my big winter coat at the entrance.

"I'll only be five minutes." I step away. "I'll be right back, I promise."

She purses her lips, as if she's thinking really hard about what she should do. "I promise," I repeat and step away from them, hurrying to the exit door. I get my hand stamped and slide past the bouncer.

I breathe in the air of Paris. It's not something specific about the city but ever since I arrived, I feel like I've been transported into this new world, this old world: the cafés on the street, the people rushing around like in New York but then still taking the time to live and argue and love. And the buildings fascinate me. Mom used to tell me stories about the architecture in Paris like she would tell me a goodnight story—full of whispers and enthralled in the legends. She loves the big avenues like this one, where the buildings have balconies wrapped around the third and sixth floor. All coming from the time Napoleon decided to redesign the city. And I could spend hours looking at them. I stroll down and turn into a side street. There the buildings appear older, a bit more cramped together. They look like they've seen it all. And they probably have. My eyes search for a possible inscription on the building in front of me. I've been taking pictures of every one I see. Like by my apartment, there's one mentioning a soldier who died during World War II and another that references a writer who lived in that house during the 18th century. I glance up at the small balcony, wondering what the history of this particular building is, who lives there, who lived there before. Anything to let go of the annoyance and sadness rippling through me.

"Bah alors t'es toute seule?"

I turn my head to the right. One guy approaches, but his smile is not friendly or flirty. His smirk has me shivering from fear instead of the cold, and my entire body tenses. I've ventured a bit far from the club and there's no one around.

I open my mouth, ready to scream, but there's a flash in the dark. The moon reflects on the blade of a knife and I freeze. I can't move. All I can think is that my parents shouldn't have to lose another daughter.

That I need to call them, talk to them, tell them how much I love them.

That I don't want to die.

CHAPTER 2 – LUCAS

I didn't want to go out tonight. I wanted to stay home and watch a movie, but Steve insisted we needed to chill before the big audition we're having for our next music video. This next song could put us back on the map or bury us deep in the charts. There's so much expectation and I don't know…I'm not feeling it.

"I don't want to talk about it." I sound annoyed, but I'm fighting hard to keep my cool. My manager—Grégoire—is on his way to the club, calling me from his cell like what he has to tell me can't wait. "Listen, I got to go. I'll see you when you get there." I hang up before he tries to guilt me into listening to him. He's pretty good at that. Playing the guilt card. Reminding me that the other members of the band depend on me. Reminding me that my best friend—Benji—lived for the music and that he wouldn't want me to give up. Reminding me that we have fans waiting for us, people who care.

But I don't feel like talking about the band tonight.

I stretch to catch another glimpse of the gorgeous girl sitting at the bar. That top she has on isn't very thick and every time she moves, it moves along with her, floating on her beautiful skin. I'm dying to run my fingers through her hair and if Bjorn—the actor who should win an award for assholery—wasn't sitting next to her, I'd make a move.

I should make a move anyways.

I stand up, but before I can walk up to her, Dimitri—another member of our band—stops me. "I'm so happy you're here," he slurs before hugging me. "I'm just so happy." He plops himself on the seat by me and wraps his arm around me. He's usually the quiet type, but when he drinks he's out of this world. And right now he's so drunk, I need to call a driver for him. His wife, Amie, will never forgive me if I let him go out like this. "We're going to be awesome. I need us to be awesome," he mutters and again I'm reminded I'm not the only one in the band. The only one who needs this. Dimitri helps Amie's entire family. He doesn't only pay the mortgage of her parents' house, he also foots the bill for his own younger brother's tuition. He got accepted into a prestigious business school in Paris, but didn't qualify for financial aid. Dimitri is only twenty-five but according to Grégoire, the way he takes care of everyone, the way he is with Amie, he appeals to a different demographic.

"I want another drink." He holds himself to the table before leaning back and closing his eyes. Snoring.

My eyes dart around. The mysterious girl is talking to the girl who's sitting with Steve, and then she slides out of the club not wearing her coat. She has to come back.

I call a driver for Dimitri and tell Steve I'm bringing him out. The girl he's with stares at my sunglasses without saying a word, and I tilt my head and pat Steve's shoulder, silently reminding him that I'm Clément tonight. Clément the roadie.

I don't want to be famous tonight.

Dimitri's heavy but at least cooperating. Once outside, the cold air has him shivering. The car pulls up soon after, and I help him inside, call Amie to let her know he's on his way. She thanks me profusely. As I talk to her, my steps take me down almost to the Seine and I stare at the reflection of the lights on the water.

So peaceful.

My phone buzzes with a text.

I'm inside the club. Where are you?

Grégoire must not be pleased, and when Grégoire is not pleased he's even more unpleasant than usual. What really pushes me to turn back around, though, is the thought that the gorgeous girl might be back at the bar. If she's gone before I get back inside, that's going to put a damper on my evening.

I stride back, enjoying being incognito for the evening, thinking about new songs for our next album even though I haven't been able to write a single song since the one about Benji's death.

But then I see her.

CHAPTER 3 - JEN

My back is pressed against the cold wall. And my brain searches for something, anything to get me out of this situation, but all I can concentrate on is the scar on his left cheek. I'm tempted to ask him where he got it from. Maybe save myself some time. Maybe show him that I'm a person too.

"Tu parles pas, t'es timide?" His breath smells like beer and hopelessness.

My limited French can't save me from this situation. *"Je...Je ne comprends pas."*

LOVE IN B MINOR

He blocks my way. "You no speak French?" He rubs his fingers together. "Money. Money."

There's someone in the distance. That's my chance. "I don't have money." My voice is loud enough for him to hear me. He turns around, and I swear he can see me, but instead of coming to help, he keeps on walking. My chest tightens; what if I don't find a way out?

My phone is tucked in my back pocket. I'd give him my purse if it only held my ID, one credit card and twenty euros. But it also has a picture of my little sister, and it's not one of those pictures that is saved on the computer or from my phone. When she was feeling better, I took her to the mall because she wanted to ride the merry-go-round there. There were those photo booths and we made silly faces and we laughed and I can't lose those pictures.

He taps on my head. "Hello? You hear?"

I stare at him and for a split second, he almost looks embarrassed, like he doesn't want to do this. I could maybe talk him out of taking my purse and hope for the best.

15

A shadow appears to my left. Nope. Not a shadow. A guy.

"Il y a un problème?" He doesn't seem scared. Or looking for a fight. Just concerned. And there's something in the way he walks that reassures me. Maybe it's the confidence or simply the fact that he seems to care. Though he's got shades on at night, so maybe I'm misreading everything.

"I'm not sure." My voice doesn't shake as much as I thought it would, and I cross my fingers he speaks English.

He steps even closer. "Are you okay?" His tone is soothing and warm, like he wants to make sure I'm not scared of him, that I know he's got my back.

"Dégage." The guy still holding the knife attempts to circle around him. Actually, while kneeing *someone* in the balls might not be a great idea, kicking *him* in the balls is an excellent idea. I focus on the movement, like I would for a pirouette; I gather all my adrenaline into that one kick and as swiftly as possible, I kick him where it hurts. He screeches loudly and bends down, jumping on his feet, dropping his knife.

LOVE IN B MINOR

"Salope. Putain, salope." Something about calling me a bitch. The guy with the sunglasses touches my shoulder.

"That was amazing," he says and then he lowers his voice just above a whisper. "You look like you could use a shot of something—you're shaking."

Before I can reply, two bouncers from the club run our way. One of them pins the mugger to the wall. The mugger who is now whimpering, and mumbling words in French I don't understand.

The other bouncer catches sight of us and his eyes widen. Words tumble out of his mouth and he sounds apologetic, but I'm not sure why.

The guy who helped me switches to English. "We should call the police."

The bouncer's mouth opens then closes. Which has me all kinds of confused as to what's going on. Finally, he speaks. "I will do that. I will tell them what happened. We have cameras out there so it should be fine. You can go back inside."

The mugger yells and thrashes but the bouncer holding him doesn't bulge.

I raise my hand as if I'm back in school—I'm feeling way too calm for what happened. "Shouldn't we wait for the police?"

The bouncer shakes his head. "Two other people have been robbed today and the police have been looking for a guy who matches this description."

"Putain, j'ai rien fait!" The robber screams and struggles to get away from the bouncer's grasp. "I didn't do nothing!" He yells this time in English as if for my benefit, as if I would take his side, defend him, say it must all be a big mistake. I stare at him. His skin is ashen and his hair is in strings like it hasn't been washed in days. His arms are strong but his cheeks are hollow like he hasn't eaten properly in weeks and his eyes are full of despair, of need. He looks like an addict who hasn't had his fix in too long. My heart beats faster than if I had danced an entire ballet. The adrenaline crashes down and I'm left with feelings I can't deal with: that fear of dying, this desire to live, is that what my little sister had to deal with before taking a last breath? Did she know what was happening? A fist of

sadness tightens around my throat. Tears threaten to escape.

The guy with the sunglasses nudges me softly as if he doesn't want to scare me, as though he can see I'm very close to losing it. "If you want to stay, we can stay. But otherwise, Karim has my number." He points to the bouncer who's been talking to us, the one who looks a bit older and very nice. "I'll make sure he'll give it to them." His voice is soothing and concerned and I'm tempted to step into his arms. I'm not making any sense.

I'm torn. I want to stay, but really, what do I have on the guy except him flashing a knife at me? He didn't put it to my throat, he didn't rob me, he threatened me but didn't touch me.

The robber is silent now, but still staring at me. Karim looks at me gruffly but with a hint of kindness. "My daughter is your age." He's got a thick French accent and I have to decipher some of the words. He pauses as if he's conflicted and then continues. "You don't need to wait. He's been operating in this area for the past three weeks, but the police are more interested about…how do you say this…the bigger fish. His boss. You…" His eyes look like a father's eyes. It's the same look I've seen in my dad's eyes when he's worried. "You don't deserve to have to wait here in the same air as the man who attacked you. Trust me, you don't need to stay."

I nod, not breaking eye contact, and the smile I give him is grateful.

The guy with the sunglasses leans in, and his breath on my neck is another reminder I'm alive. "Come on, let me get you back inside."

I wave at Karim, manage to tell him *"Merci"* while the robber leans against the wall, having apparently decided that being silent was better for him than the insults he was throwing in the wind.

And then I turn to Sunglasses. "Thank you. I didn't even thank you." The words jump out of my mouth uncoordinated, which isn't usual for me. All I want to do is get away now, get away from here, from everything. "This evening hasn't gone as planned," I mumble and my voice sound like I'm in shock and why am I saying this out loud?

LOVE IN B MINOR

Sunglasses' hand finds the small of my back and warmth spreads everywhere. He gently guides me away—back toward the entrance of the club, as if he knows how close I am to completely losing it. There's a chuckle in his voice, almost a reassuring chuckle, when he answers and he almost has no French accent—more American than anything else. "You mean getting robbed wasn't part of your plans?"

"Nope."

His sunglasses are still firmly seated on his nose, and even though I find that strange in the middle of the night, I don't want to mention it. Maybe he has a disease, maybe he feels self-conscious, maybe he has a thing for sunglasses. Who am I to judge? I've learned the hard way how appearances can be deceiving.

His smile is mesmerizing and for a split second, I'm tempted to ask him if he wants to get out of here. Not sure if it's the adrenaline or the need to prove to myself that I'm alive, but going home with this guy doesn't sound crazy.

I shiver and my teeth chatter once, twice and then rapidly. And I wince, thinking of the image I must give: scared, lost, and without a jacket like some careless person.

"Here." He takes off his winter jacket and places it carefully over my shoulders. "Let me take you back inside. I'm sure your friend is wondering where you are."

"My friend? How did you know I was inside?"

Hi s hands are still on my shoulders and when he takes them away, I feel cold again. His voice is still full of warmth, maybe warmer than before. "I saw you in there. I was about to ask you if you wanted a drink when Bjorn sat next to you."

How did I not notice him? He's not only tall, but he's got this dark and handsome vibe that I usually crave. As if he could read my thoughts he continues, "I was sitting in the back."

"Oh." And then because I told myself tonight was going to be a good night and because I think he could make it a good night, I tilt my head to the side and say, "I wouldn't mind another drink. But I also wouldn't mind having another drink somewhere else."

LOVE IN B MINOR

He chuckles and his mouth curves up into a knowing smile that gives the sleepy butterflies in my stomach a kick and wakes them up. He extends his hand to me. "I'm…" He pauses as if waiting for me to say something, and when I don't he continues—a bit more hesitant. "I'm Clément."

I take his hand in mine. His hand is warm and strong and rough. The butterflies in my stomach spread their wings and stretch happily. "I'm Laura."

I used the same fake name during my first week in Paris. Before I started at the ballet company. I needed to get out of my head and I did. The guy I met that night was nice, but we didn't have anything in common except a desire to land in my bed. Which we did, and I never saw him again.

I need to convince myself that it's the same with Clément. He may be sexy and he may have saved me, but he's just that. A one-night stand.

"I need my coat and to say bye to my friend."

Clément brings my hand to his lips and softly presses his mouth to each of my knuckles. The air shifts, full of desire and tension, and I forget everything that's not him. He could lean in to kiss me right now—I would not push him away. But instead, he breaks the silence. "I'll wait for you out here."

I shuffle out of his coat, hurry back inside, grab my coat at the concierge and make my way to Alisha. The music seems louder, pounding in my veins. The smells seem more pronounced, making me dizzy. The crowd seem larger, trapping me.

I stop and hold myself at the bar, breathing in and out. After a few seconds, my head is less fuzzy and the beating of my heart is less erratic. Bjorn the Actor is alone again—I guess even the girl who seemed so hung up on him couldn't deal with his nonexistent conversation. He hasn't spotted me yet but his eyes scan the room and I don't want to be found. I stride through the crowd. Alisha's still sitting with Steve, still laughing and having a great time, it seems. "I'm leaving."

"With the dude with sunglasses?"

"What?" How can she know that already?

"He works with Steve," she explains, nudging Steve, who stares into his beer. "He's a roadie, I think."

LOVE IN B MINOR

"He's a roadie, helps the band with all the technical stuff," he mutters.

"What band is it?" I ask but Alisha shakes her head.

"He doesn't want to say, apparently it's a big secret. Not sure it's even true," she teases and Steve pulls her closer to him. Clearly, he's enjoying his time with her, and me staying here is putting a damper on their alone-time. "Will you text me later though? Let me know you're okay."

"You do the same."

She nods and I almost skip out of the club.

The dance floor smells like expensive perfume mixed with sweat. Because even money doesn't stop you from sweating. Even though my mood still isn't the brightest, or maybe because my mood is all over the place, I almost giggle at myself. It's not the alcohol because I only drank that half mojito…but maybe tonight I can let anything and everything happen if I want to.

It's a parenthesis.

Not real life.

CHAPTER 4 - LUCAS

I text Grégoire that I'm leaving and will see him soon and don't pick up when he calls. Not wanting to hear how disappointed he is. Not in the mood to hear how careless I'm being with everything that's at stake. My eyes keep glancing to the door, waiting for Laura to appear. Spending time with her tonight definitely beats listening to Grégoire. And she doesn't seem to know who I am, which is a relief.

Karim—the bouncer—comes back to where I stand. "I wanted to let you know the police are on their way and we'll keep you updated."

LOVE IN B MINOR

"Thanks. I appreciate it." If I can avoid being seen with the police right now, it would be great. I don't need one new headline spreading lies about me.

He's about to say something else, when Laura steps outside. She's got a hat on and a big winter jacket; looking all warm and cozy. She glances up at me and her lips curve into a smile. And I could get lost into that smile.

And I need to stop staring at her lips. "You're ready? I know this little bar close to the Eiffel Tower. We can call a cab or we can walk." I eye her heels with one raised eyebrow because I'm always wondering how women can walk in those.

"I'd love to walk," she replies and links her arm in mine. Whatever awkwardness I was afraid of, there's none. "I haven't seen a lot of Paris and I've been here for four months."

"What brought you to Paris?"

She glances at me and pauses as if she's thinking hard about her answer. "I'm here to learn French." We stop at a light, but since there's no car, I tug her to cross the street. "I've noticed Parisian and

27

New Yorkers are similar in a lot of ways." She chuckles. "Like crossing streets when you probably shouldn't. And they do love their city. Where are you from?"

I bring her closer to me so she avoids some poop left on the sidewalk. Paris may be gorgeous, but it's not Berlin when it comes to cleanliness. "All over the place. Mainly, Maine and Paris."

"Thank you again so much for coming to help me. There was a guy before you who passed by without doing anything."

"People are assholes."

"I would agree with that statement." Her eyes dart everywhere, and she's got a thoughtful smile on her face. "Can you imagine the French Revolution happening here? Every place I come across is full of history and meaning."

"Do you like history?"

She nods with a dreamy smile and stops to touch a plaque on one building. "What does this one say? I can understand some people met here, but I'm not sure of the rest."

LOVE IN B MINOR

"It says that in September 1944, the forces of the Résistance met in this building."

She grabs her phone out of her back pocket to snap a picture. My body tenses at the flash. What if she did recognize me and is only playing a game?

And clearly, Steve is right when he says I have issues. Not everyone is out there to use me. I force myself to relax.

She turns to me and she gives me that smile again. A few smiles and she's got me hooked, but it's the passion in her voice that leaves me wanting more. "I love history. I've always loved it. I have four ways to deal with stress. I dance," she explains.

"You dance?"

She swats her hand in the air like it's not a big deal. "You know, silly dances in the kitchen."

And I can picture her dancing in my kitchen. Not wearing a lot. I shake my head—clearly not the moment to think about her naked. "I watch Netflix. I imagine what people wore and said centuries ago, like making up stories in my mind." She chuckles and her entire face brightens. "I have never said that to anyone."

"Your secret is safe with me." We make our way toward the Seine. To get to that bar, we're going to cross one of Paris's many bridges. The wind blows in gusts and I try to walk in the way that I can act as windshield. "You mentioned four ways of dealing with stress. How about the last one?"

She bumps her hip with mine. "Spending a magical evening with a pretty nice guy."

"Pretty nice guy, huh?" We step onto the bridge. And even though the wind is still pretty strong, she stops in the middle.

"This is absolutely gorgeous." She breathes the words out like if she says them too loudly she's going to break the moment.

And I see it. Even though Paris is my second home, I see the amazement. The view of the Eiffel Tower from the Pont de l'Alma is breathtaking. A few groups of people pass us and I pull my beanie further down. But they don't recognize me. Nowadays, I'm more famous in the gossip magazines for my random hookups than for my music. But that should change with our next release.

"I could spend hours here. Looking at it. I never thought iron could have that effect on me." She tilts her head toward me and I'm tempted to lean in and kiss her, but instead I simply wrap my arms around her. She settles against me as if we've done this many times before, and now I could also stay like this for hours.

She still stares ahead—and I wonder what thoughts she lost herself to, when she speaks. She sounds lost in her world. "Did you know that in 1963, French television recorded an amazing ballet on the fourth floor of the Eiffel Tower? My mom showed me once—it was with Zizi Jeanmaire."

This time, I'm the one chuckling, not surprised at what she knows but amazed by how in awe she sounds. I've missed that. Finding someone to be in awe with. I lower my head into the nook of her neck and this time when she shivers, I'm not sure it's from the cold. "Can we walk all the way to the Eiffel Tower?" she asks, her voice slightly huskier than before.

"Whatever you want."

Because right here, right now, if she asked me for the moon, I might try to find a way to bring it down. I don't know her, not really, but it feels like I do.

CHAPTER 5 – JEN

After spending a few more minutes watching the Eiffel Tower, we stroll hand in hand through the almost-empty streets of Paris. Some drunk people are partying but it's mostly quiet. When we get to the Eiffel Tower, we plop ourselves on an empty bench.

"It is…magical," I whisper. Everything about this night is magical—not counting the douchebag and the almost-robbery.

"Is this the first time you've seen it at night?" he asks, sounding surprised, and I understand since it's one of the first monument people flock to, day and night.

"Not the first time I've seen it, but it's the first time I've taken the time to look." I shrug. "I don't know if I make sense."

He leans in. "You make a lot of sense." His lips are close to my cheek and he softly kisses it. I'm about to melt like the last snow on the trees. His voice is strong and sexy. I never thought a voice could be sexy. But clearly, that was before, because I could listen to him for hours.

His hand reaches up and I think he's going to cup my face and bring me closer and finally kiss me, but instead he takes off his sunglasses.

And since he seems to be fine without them, I take the plunge. "So, were you wearing those to hide from a jealous ex?" I almost wink but somehow my brain manages to tell my body this is a bad idea.

His laugh is the most restrained I've heard all night, like a tame version of himself. But then, our eyes collide. And for the very first time I understand what it

means to get lost in someone's eyes. It isn't the color—
I don't see any specks of gold, or the ocean in them,
they're just dark blue—but it's the intensity in them
that gets my breath to hitch.

"My name is Burt Macklin. I work for the FBI."

A giggle burst outs...I never giggle...But *Parks
& Rec* is one of the only shows I actually binge-
watched last summer on Netflix and if I believed in
signs, I'd say him quoting my favorite show is exactly
that. A sign. "Really? Next, you're going to tell me
you're a musician and that your name is…"

He tilts his head. "What? What's my name?"
His lips are too close for me to form one coherent
thought, so I lean back.

"Johnny Karate, of course." I almost don't
recognize my voice. It's too soft, too sweet, too smooth.

And his laughter booms in the quiet night. And
seeing him laugh makes me want to smile right along
with him. And I want to hold on to that feeling a bit
longer. One of my hands slowly reaches out and my
fingers trail down his cheek while my other hand falls
on his knee. He stops laughing. His gaze turns hungry.

"I'm not really thirsty anymore," I whisper. Our eyes lock. The tension crackling between us gets even more intense. He leans in and I hold my breath. We're lost in the moment, in the anticipation, in that one second. That one second before a first kiss. I bridge the tiny distance between us and when our lips meet, I breathe again.

His lips are strong and soft.

My body melts into his despite the layers. One of his hands caresses my back and I press myself against him, wishing I could feel his skin against mine. His tongue slips inside my mouth, teasing mine into a playful dance. His other hand cups my face and I could stay like this forever. But I want more. And what I have in mind probably shouldn't happen outside.

We might get arrested.

But I don't want to end the night here and now.

I don't want this night to end at all.

CHAPTER 6 - LUCAS

She breaks away, but her smile isn't apologetic or telling me she wants to stop—her smile is almost a promise for more. "I'm not thirsty, but I am hungry. Any chance you know how to cook?"

I raise an eyebrow, keeping an arm around her. "I'm not bad. I can make mean pasta."

"How about cookies?"

"Cookies?" Laughter rumbles deep in my chest. I can't remember the last time I baked cookies. I also can't remember the last time I had such a wonderful time. She plants a soft kiss on my lips.

"Cookies," she confirms. "I've got a craving for cookies. I'll help you."

"I'm not even sure if I have chocolate chips." I pause and check my phone. It's past midnight, the little Monoprix by my apartment closes at midnight, and I can't think of any other stores that are open. But then I remember. "Wait, I might. Mom loves to put chocolate chips in her oatmeal with bananas. Don't ask me why."

"That actually sounds delicious!" she replies with a smile that continues to move things inside me I wasn't sure still existed.

"So, wait. Am I really about to bake cookies in the middle of the night?"

She bites the side of her lower lip. "If you don't mind me coming over." She sounds unsure, or maybe a bit weirded out, and then I realize what I said could mean I live with my mom and that would be fifty shades of awkward.

"You know, my mom…" I rush to continue. "She doesn't live with me. I don't live with her. She sometimes comes to visit. And that's where the chocolate chips come in."

LOVE IN B MINOR

Her eyes light up and her smile is definitely less restrained, as if she's relieved, and she laughs. And then she must see how much I want her because she stops laughing, but there's still a hint of a smile. A very sexy smile.

I pull her to me and kiss her again.

I kiss her senseless.

Because for once, I'm not sure I want this night to end.

For once, having a one-night stand doesn't feel right.

Doesn't feel true.

In the morning, I'll tell her my real name. I'll tell her everything.

CHAPTER 7 – JEN

The smell of freshly baked cookies floats in the air—a tempting and teasing reminder of last night. But even though I'm worried my stomach is going to rumble, I don't move. I stare at the ceiling, same as I've been doing the past ten minutes, and continue to will the knots of tension braided through my body to unwind.

It's the first time since I've arrived in Paris that I don't wake up in my apartment.

And I'm definitely not in my apartment.

This place is an open loft: too bright, too big, too homey. Books, a mix of encyclopedias and what seem to be thrillers, line the shelves, a grand piano stands in the middle of the living room, and a giant poster of a piano competition decorates one side of the wall, while on the other side, there is a poster of the Badgers football team, and of a soccer team. I squint to read the words. It's the French national soccer team.

My walls are bare except for drawings my sister did for me while at the hospital. The lump in my throat that lingers whenever I think of my sister is there, but for once it's not overpowering. And I can't cry in some almost-stranger's bed.

Even though after last night, he doesn't feel like a stranger.

I bite the inside of my cheek, hold my breath and slowly, very slowly turn my head to the left.

Random guy I met for the first time yesterday? Check.

Random *hot* guy who made feel like I've known him forever? Double check.

Random *hot* guy sleeping on his back with the covers barely covering him making my heart pound? Triple check.

I have to force myself not to trail my fingers from his large shoulders, down his rock-hard abs. That might wake him up and defeat my attempt to gracefully and quietly slip away. His dark hair is tousled and his stubble probably left marks on my neck and many other places. My face flushes. Even asleep, he's got that little something that sends the most delicious shivers down my spine.

And if I keep on staring, he's going to wake up.

Can't happen.

I force myself to look away,

The sweet aroma tickles my nose again.

Memories of last night rush back to me, how I dared a guy I had known for about two hours to bake me cookies. And he did. And man, those cookies were amazing. Soft and chewy and chocolaty. Like the perfect—

A strong arm curls over my waist and cuts off my thoughts.

This should feel weird and unfamiliar.

It doesn't.

LOVE IN B MINOR

I shouldn't want to cuddle closer, to keep my eyes closed and play pretend.

I do.

And for a second, I picture leaning into his strong arms, burying my face in the crook of his neck, letting myself believe that what we had last night meant more than it does. That it could be more than a one-night stand.

But I learned long ago not to believe in fairy tales.

I clench my muscles, every fiber of my body resisting the temptation to slide closer to him, and I roll over on my side, slowly and carefully.

Last night was my first night of real fun in Paris after a crappy start. I've never thought that I could be more myself by pretending to be someone else. But last night I found myself laughing again. Even though I wasn't supposed to end up here. I was supposed to go out, let off some steam, not almost get robbed, not hook up with some random guy.

He may have been my knight in shining armor and be a Master of Amazing Cookies, but he doesn't want to get involved with me. Hell, sometimes I don't want to be involved with me and I'm stuck with me. He has a choice.

I scoot to the side of the king-size bed, my heart in my throat. The floor creaks under my feet, and I hold my breath but he doesn't move.

My clothes are scattered on the floor. I find one piece at a time, but my shirt is nowhere to be seen. Not on the counter where the cookie batter still stands. Not on the piano. Not on the large shelves. My eyes catch a picture of Clément with two other people at Disneyland Paris. He's got the biggest smile and his arms are wrapped around a tall blond guy and a girl. A beautiful girl with almost translucent skin and reddish hair. Pretty much my opposite. I twist my dark black hair into a messy bun and continue to search for my ruby top—the one that's supposed to help me fake it until I believe it.

Fake smile. Fake having fun. Fake everything.

Except I didn't have to fake anything with him last night. Not my laugh, not my silences, not…anything.

I place the frame back in its place.

LOVE IN B MINOR

Please, tell me he doesn't have a girlfriend. Please tell me that I'm not the other woman. I've seen how my friend Emilia's mom suffered from being lied to for years. I don't think I could deal with the guilt. My heart deflates back into its sad state, but there's nothing I can do about it now, except find my shirt.

I close my eyes, retracing my steps into the loft.

He pulls me to him and I kiss him first. My lips are desperate. My skin is on fire. His hands are on my back, on my ass, everywhere. He whispers in my ear, asking me to stay, letting go of me, giving me a way out. A way out I don't want to take. I step back to take a better look at him. His face falls, and he mutters something about wanting to see me again, and wanting to call me a cab or something. And I bite the inside of my cheek to not smile. I slowly take off my ruby backless top, throwing it to the other side of the counter.

And that's where I find it.

The sun filters through the light curtains.

He sighs loudly, mutters something, and I stop breathing. I so do not want the awkward good morning and even more awkward "do we kiss or hug or shake hands" type of situation.

He lays on his other side now and the tattoo on his arm is more visible—it's a tattoo of two birds flying side by side. He mentioned something yesterday about how it's important to always remember to live. That those birds were his reminder to always remember to live every second. We sure did yesterday.

My stomach rumbles more loudly than Igor— my ballet company's director—when he yells at me to deepen my extension. Not sure if it's the cookies, or the smell of the pizza he convinced me to eat last night. The box is still on the table.

Tempting me. Teasing me.

Like him.

But I can't stay. I don't even leave a note. To him, I'm Laura Smith. The fake name I used once before—my very first week in Paris, when an Irish guy hit on me in a restaurant and I was so sad I thought he could make me feel alive. He didn't.

And while with Clément it felt different, there's no need to pretend we're more than a one-night stand.

LOVE IN B MINOR

I put on my coat, force myself to not look at him one more time because my resolve seems to be as crumbly as those cookies, and head out into the biting January cold.

His apartment is close to the Eiffel Tower. In the early morning, the Iron Lady isn't surrounded by tourists taking pictures, hurrying to go up the stairs and waiting by the elevators. Much different from last night.

I sit on a bench.

I only need a second to breathe. To remind myself why I'm here, what I'm doing.

My thoughts are scrambled up despite the fact that I kept to my one-cocktail rule. I can't afford the crazy calories. I'm not sure if it's the lack of sleep, or the piece of pizza, or sitting in the cold morning in Paris, but I'm thinking maybe cuddling with the guy I spent a wonderful night with would not have been the worst decision of my life.

I know for a fact it wouldn't be the worst decision of my life.

I settle on the bench and inhale deeply, the freezing air slamming into my lungs. I push away any thought that isn't about this moment. My fingers trace the names engraved on the bench and my stupid happy smile is back. We made out on a bench similar to this one last night.

Cars honk in the distance and a gust of wind sneaks under the coat I forgot to close. I shake my head both at my past self for being so lost in the moment and my present self for turning into such a daydreamer. I don't have time for this, I don't have the energy.

A group of students must have decided to brave both the wind and the early hour. They stroll toward the Eiffel Tower, pushing each other, laughing, talking in a language I don't understand. The people selling souvenirs trickle in, setting up. They look tired—they were louder yesterday, faking that they were happy to be there too.

It's time to go home and forget this night ever happened.

I shuffle through my bag. Where the heck is my phone? My heart accelerates. Maybe I forgot it at his place. Maybe it's a sign I need to turn back around and enjoy being Laura for a few more hours. Maybe…

LOVE IN B MINOR

My fingers find my phone tucked into one of the side pockets.

Maybe it's not meant to be. I sigh.

There are two text messages, and for one split second I almost hope my parents remembered they had another daughter. I wrote them another email yesterday.

But the first one is from my friend Emilia from the School of Performing Arts in New York. *Culinary arts is as cutthroat as ballet. I swear...someone just mixed sugar with salt. Ridiculous. How are you doing? How is Paris? And yes I know you don't want to hear it, but I miss you!*

I'd love to write back and tell her about Clément, how hard it has been, how much harder the ballet company is than the School. How much more competitive. I'd love to tell her I miss her too, but I hold back. Like I always do.

Because if I did talk to Em, I'd break down. We've come a long way in the past two years, from sworn enemies to actual friends.

I distract myself—which is another thing I've become a pro at.

I read Alisha's new message—she sent it almost an hour ago, which means she's been up since at least six a.m. Alisha is one of the only two girls at the ballet company I trust not to make me trip and fall to get a better part. *Get away from Sexy Sunglasses guy and get your cute butt to my room asap. I heard about an audition last night from Steve. And you need to come with me.*

She knows we can't dance anywhere else. The contract we signed at the beginning of the year mentioned exclusivity with the company, and she's usually so good at sticking with the rules.

I type back, my fingers almost uncooperative because of the cold. *I don't think we should.*

Oh come on, it would be fun. And different. Her reply comes immediately. *By the way, how was the rest of your night? So relieved you're typing back and not holed up in some cave with a serial killer.*

Alive and well. How was your night?

Her answer takes a bit longer. *It was nice.*

That's it? Steve didn't sweep you off your feet?

LOVE IN B MINOR

And then when she doesn't answer, I frown—worried something might have happened despite her texting me at one that she was leaving the club. *Alisha, are you okay?*

☺ *I'm fine. Don't worry. I just don't think Steve is going to be thrilled to see me at that audition if we do go. I may have left in a hurry.*

I'm heading home. I'll pass by your place later this afternoon?

Sounds good.

Maybe I'll even take a nap, which I haven't done in forever, but after last night I'm left with a weird mix of renewed energy and relaxed laziness. Like I'm content and ready to take on the world.

I keep on staring at the Eiffel Tower.

My phone beeps again. A text from Audrey, the secretary of the ballet company. *Emergency meeting at 10 am in the studio. Don't be late. It's mandatory. Igor has an announcement.*

This can't be good.

MARIAN J MOHR LIBRARY

CHAPTER 8 – LUCAS

I hate the awkward morning-after routine. I hate the small talk. I hate when the girl's eyes are full of hope I'm going to crush. Even if I didn't mean to, even if I told her I wasn't looking for anything, even if I never make false promises. Seeing the hurt replace the hope is the worse.

Benji—Benjamin—my bromance, as the tabloids called us, would probably have told me I don't need to act like a dick all the time. And he would probably have been right, but ever since he's been gone, nothing has been the same. And the girl I thought

LOVE IN B MINOR

I was going to spend my entire life with not only broke my heart, she used me. I got burned badly, and the scars haven't totally healed.

So, yes, I slept around. Or to be even more honest, I fucked. A lot. But I never lied. My motto is to be upfront. But I know I've hurt people despite that policy, because it seems people still want to believe they can change you, make you into what they think you should be. Whatever that means.

I can almost hear Benji telling me that's the universe coming back to bite me in the ass.

Because today, the other side of my bed is cold.

Way too cold.

Laura is the first girl I ever brought here…maybe because she didn't recognize me, or maybe because I haven't laughed so much in what seems like years, or maybe because I wanted to keep her to myself a bit longer.

She's gone.

I turn to look around, but the apartment is silent.

Usually, I'd feel relieved. I'd get up, take a shower, get to work. But instead, I sit up and rake my hand through my hair. The cookies I baked are on the table next to the pizza I ordered.

The reality hits me right in the gut and I'm tempted to laugh. I baked cookies.

I can't fucking believe I baked cookies.

I also can't believe how baking cookies ended up being so sexy. Her hands finding mine in the dough, me feeding her, her laughing.

I yawn and stretch, grab sweatpants lying by the side of the bed. Out of habit, I check to see if she left me anything: a composite of her for an audition, a USB stick with some demo music. Checking if she played me. But there's nothing.

Even though the groupies who follow us from city to city are usually more into the rush of sleeping with someone they think is famous, there are some who slip me a USB with a demo of them singing, or a card with their numbers to give to a casting director. I don't mix my private life with business. I'm also upfront about that. Magazines wonder when I'm going to settle down, but according to Grégoire, my bad boy image definitely helps my career. That and the rumor he keeps on spreading that me and my ex could get back together.

It would appear that getting your heart broken is a wonderful way to boost sales.

And man, my ex—Olivia—did break my heart. I still can't believe I was such an idiot.

I rub the back of my neck. Last night I wasn't Lucas Wills; last night I was more myself than ever before. I grab a cookie and it melts in my mouth. Laura was so impressed with my cooking skills. And I was so impressed with her. My eyes scan the room—the empty box of pizza, the newspapers on the counter, the piano. I put away the dishes, not able to shake her from my mind. Google could be my friend. I usually avoid it like the dealers who hang at the A-list parties. Too many risks of seeing bullshit written about me. Too many risks of reading about my ex and her lies about me. Too many risks of hearing a new theory about Benji and why he died.

It always slices my heart.

I type maybe a bit too strongly on the keyboard. "Laura Smith." She said she was here to learn French. There are more than thirty-three million results.

Frustration finds a comfy spot in my chest, makes itself as comfortable as a reporter who doesn't want to leave. Frustration I can't even begin to understand.

She's just a girl.

But a girl with a contagious laugh and a ridiculously adorable snort.

I grab my cell phone and dial Steve's number— he was hanging out with one of her friends. Maybe he knows about where she could be, or who she is.

His hello is barely a grunt.

"Hey, what's up?"

"You're calling me." His voice is gruff—a testimony to the fact the guy could sleep until two if we let him and he still would say it's too early.

"You hung out with a girl last night. Tall, blonde…"

"And you never came back. Grégoire was beyond pissed, dude."

LOVE IN B MINOR

"I'm allowed a night off." Annoyance ripples through me. Grégoire has been our manager since he discovered Benji, Olivia and me at a school function. He decided we would become the next "it" band and added Dimitri to the mix. He did manage to turn us into an overnight sensation. And ever since the band "took a break" (his words, not mine), after Benji's death, he's been on my case to make the perfect comeback. I clench my fist on my thigh, trying to calm myself. "Everything is set up anyways. We do the fucking video, and our concert is already booked. I don't know what he wants."

"Whatever… Don't kill the messenger." He grunts louder. "It's fucking seven in the morning on a Sunday."

"The girl, Steve," I remind him and then smooth my voice, needing to bribe him with something. "I can get coffee delivered to your place if you want."

Steve can't live without his daily dose of Starbucks Latte Macchiato. He says it reminds him of home. Grégoire had this big "Become the next member of Dire Blue" contest and Steve won. Even though I was skeptical at first and know he can never fully replace Benji, he's become part of the family.

There's shuffle on the line. He clears his throat—he probably smoked way too much last night again. "Now, you're talking. The girl I was trying to woo was tall, blonde, totally hot." He pauses. "Not your type, I know. I swear the way she kissed was such a turn-on. But she bailed on me. We were having a great time. Her friend was hot too, so I get the appeal. I know you left with her, because she told Alisha she was leaving with the guy with the sunglasses." He coughs one time. "Shit, I really should stop smoking. Anyways, I can't believe you lied to her about who you are. They seemed cool and I hate having to lie for you."

"You know Grégoire wants that first music video to be your very first public appearance so…everything is orchestrated to the tiniest detail." I sigh and lean back. "Anyways, the girls. What do you know about them?"

"Alisha is a dancer. I told her about the auditions tomorrow."

"And her friend? Laura? Is she a dancer too?"

LOVE IN B MINOR

"Laura? I don't think that was her name."

I shake my head to myself. Of course not. "What was her name?" And what else did she lie about? Not that I can judge.

"I don't know. To be honest, I was kind of focused on Alisha. Who bailed on me as I said. As soon as I suggested going back to my place, she mumbled something and left me dry." He snickers. "My balls are probably still blue."

"Wait, you went home alone?"

"I did." He sighs the longest sigh, and he's usually Mister Optimism—that girl must have done a number on him. "Such a wasted night." He chuckles but it's forced. "Anyways, why do you ask? You did go home with her friend." He mumbles, and I'm not sure if it's because he went home alone or because he's hungover. "Do you know who her friend reminded me of?"

"Who?"

"Like she could be the cousin of that singer Jhené Aiko?"

"Who?" The name sounds familiar, but I don't remember what she looks like.

"You know, Jhené. Gorgeous voice, beautiful. Fucking beautiful. I think she's half Japanese, half African-American… She's drop-dead gorgeous. Like that girl you went home with last night." He pauses like he does when he's thinking hard about something— usually about the best melody to go with a song…or about the ins and outs of engineering. Even though he cultivates his image of music sensation, he graduated early with a degree in Chemical Engineering, becoming the first one in his family to graduate college. "You did go home with her, right?"

"I did. She left before I woke up."

His laugh booms, followed by a loud grunt. "Fucking shit. My head is killing me. Don't make me laugh."

"That's not funny. She left without leaving anything behind. No note, no nothing. Like last night didn't happen."

LOVE IN B MINOR

"That's usually the way you roll though…" He sounds like Benji, and the pain of losing my best friend crashes into me. Just thinking about Benji still hurts.

"Usually." I lean back, resisting the urge to tell him to mind his own business. I called him. I asked for help. I reached out. It's not his fault.

His laugh is more subdued now but definitely more real. "She's the one-night stand who got away."

"Fuck off." I hang up to the sound of his laugh.

My phone beeps shortly after. *You're Lucas Clément Wills, you'll get the girl.*

And maybe he's right.

But maybe this time, my name won't get me any nearer to the goal.

My brain replays every moment of last night. Every smile, every laugh, every touch.

Her friend's a dancer. What if she's one too?

A dancer. She could be a dancer. She looked like a dancer: in the way she walked, in the way she got me mesmerized with every movement. After all, she lied about her name—she probably lied about that too.

Maybe she lied about everything. Maybe she did recognize me.

I want to scream. I used to trust people so easily, but Olivia really did a number on me.

I didn't want to go to those auditions tomorrow. But now I have to. I have to see her again. If her friend goes, maybe she will too.

Steve's words rush back to me. "The one-night stand who got away."

And for the first time in months, I sit at the lonely piano standing in the middle of the room. We used to come up with songs here, but now it's only collecting dust. When my fingers touch the keys, the weight of Benji's senseless death smashes into me all over me again.

But I inhale deeply, forget the dissonance screaming with each beat of my heart, and play the melody running through my mind. This melody isn't happy, it's not gritty or loud or in your face. It's sad and hopeful. It's a soundtrack of last night, it's a soundtrack of the doubts, and the pain, and finally of the hope.

Words fill my mind. A song forms in my head.

LOVE IN B MINOR

And my lips turn up into one of those smiles the press calls mysterious when I write its title: "The One-Night Stand Who Got Away."

CHAPTER 9 - JEN

Even though my tiny apartment isn't very welcoming with its bare walls and gray coloring, my big fluffy bed looks oh so inviting, but no time for a nap. I need a shower. I need to change. I need to stop thinking about Clément.

The warm water unwinds my muscles, but it does nothing to clear my mind. I lean my head against the door and turn to the mirror. The fog makes everything blurry and my reflection almost looks surreal. Sometimes, that's how I feel. As if life is passing me by. As if I can't press pause. As if I simply don't know how to live in the present.

Which is weird.

And strange.

And doesn't make any sense.

I've learned the hard way that the little moments are what matter most: seeing my sister smile as I danced for her at the hospital, hearing her laugh when Mom read her a story making the different voices, having one more day with her.

I wipe the fog away, focusing on my eyes. When I was little, I asked Mom why our eyes didn't look the same as all my friends'. I asked because a little boy at school told me my eyes looked stupid and that when I laughed, it looked like I was sleeping, while another told me my eyes didn't look as Asian.

Whatever that meant to him. Mom squatted down to my level, gently caressed my face and said that everyone looks different, but everyone has love in their hearts.

I believed her then. Not so much now.

When she told Dad, he laughed his booming laugh, the one that transformed his usually serious face into total happiness, and he hugged me saying stupidity can be found anywhere, but that I needed to remember I was his beautiful and smart little girl.

But I screwed up in so many ways. Despite all of that, they never stopped looking at me with love… Dad always said that making mistakes was part of living and that learning was the important factor. He always made sure to be there for me, but ever since Mia died, they both simply disappeared.

They work long hours.

They don't talk.

They stopped hoping.

They almost separated—they have no idea I overheard them one night when Mia was still at the hospital. They were fighting, angry about everything, quarreling about the smallest things. How the trip to France that last summer was a stupid idea, how Dad never closes the toothpaste. In the middle of the argument, they both broke down and cried.

LOVE IN B MINOR

They're still together, but it's even harder now that Mia is gone.

I pull my hair away from my face, apply some makeup.

I need to focus on the "here and now." I can't take back yesterday or the day before or the years before that. I can't change what happened no matter how I wish I could dance away the pain. But I can do something about my future.

And my future is all about forgetting my past, moving on. Shit, moving to France was part of the big plan, making sure my past doesn't come back to haunt me. But it's there, in my mind, eating at me, eating away the present.

My breathing is shallow. My hands clam up and my chest constricts. My heart speeds up and I want to scream. I recognize all the signs and it's clear I should call my therapist in New York to get a referral for someone here in Paris.

I lean against the bathroom door.

I almost hear my sister telling me it's going to be okay, and I struggle to not let the sadness overpower every cell of my being.

I inhale slowly, exhale loudly.

Tired of hiding. Tired of pretending.

After a few minutes, the wave of emotions that was crushing me subsides. I wipe away the fog with a shaking hand. Time to put the Resting Bitch Face on…the one that makes it seem like I have everything under control even though I'm spiraling.

Being in Clément's arms last night was only a parenthesis, a nice break. Nothing more.

But as soon as I'm dressed in comfy jazz pants and a loose shirt, I take a few more minutes to search his name on my phone. Clément. Roadie. Way too many hits.

The sky outside my window is white, full of heavy clouds, and it seems like it's going to snow again. My eyes glance again to the comfy bed with warm comforters and throw pillows I could bury myself under, but I clench my teeth in resolve, grab my bag, put on my boots and my winter coat, and hurry out the door.

The dance company is right around the corner. The smell of warm bread and croissants, wafts through the air coming from the bakery next to the dance company, reminds me I haven't eaten anything yet. All the pastries in the windows—macarons, almond-chocolate croissants, apple pie and more—are oh so inviting, and I do need coffee. I push the door to the bakery and a bell rings.

"*Bonjour*!" The lady at the counter sounds happy.

"Bonjour," I reply and her smile widens. She probably noticed my accent.

"*Cela.*" I point to a raspberry macaron. "And café."

"*Noir, café au lait, espresso*?" she asks, showing me each choices.

"Café au lait, please."

I wait to be outside to bite into my macaron and I almost moan out loud. This is the most delicious macaron I've ever had, and it might not be the best idea after all the pizza and cookies I had last night, but I need the sugar rush and the coffee before facing Igor again.

Starting in a company, I knew I wouldn't receive any favors, but it's still a learning process to go from being the lead in a showcase to paying your dues by dancing smaller roles. I am learning a lot, not only about dancing but also about myself and it only reinforces how much dancing means to me, how much I want to dance.

I stride inside the courtyard of our building. It always amazes me to see it—like being tucked inside Paris, full of secrets and history. Our building dates from the 17th century. Not the oldest building in Paris, which I've read is in the 3rd arrondissement. Most of the dancers from our company are already here, milling around, smoking, drinking coffee like me. The sun is out, so even though it's still cold, standing outside feels good.

I spot Alisha away from the small crowd, a cigarette between her fingers. She waves at me and I join her. Alisha blows smoke away to the other side. "It's my last one."

"You say that every single time."

Alisha has quit smoking at least ten times since I met her five months ago. "This time I mean it." She drags on her cigarette again and closes her eyes. "I know it's basically cancer on a stick but..." She winces. "I'm sorry... I didn't mean to..." She looks at me and I can sense another apology coming. Everyone at the company knows about my sister. I got an extension when they offered me a spot, and I left for a week when it was time for the funeral.

"I know." I stare at her cigarette. It's been four years since I smoked last, and my fingers still itch sometimes. But I turn away. I speak through the lump in my throat. Pretend. I can pretend to be fine, to only care about one thing. Shit, it's been the main reason I'm still active, still doing something. Dancing saved me from myself, but sometimes there is a part of me that wonders if it's only a smoke screen.

Instead of going crazy asking myself questions I have no answer for, I lean against the wall next to her.

"What's that audition you were talking about? Do we even have time? And how are we going to manage to do it?" I take a deep breath. Finally calmer. "It does go against the contract."

"I'm not entirely sure; we can't dance for another ballet company while we're employed here, and we have to avoid activities that could result in injuries, but technically we could stretch the rules."

"You never stretch the rules."

"And you always said you wanted to make a career out of dancing. What Steve told me is that they need to make a splash with this new video. He said something about the band banking everything on that music video." She pauses, drags another puff of her cigarette as if she isn't sure if she should enjoy it or hate it. "He still didn't want to tell me the name of the band. Apparently it's very hush-hush. I Googled it and there were a few articles about super big names like Villain Complex."

"Aren't they touring right now?"

LOVE IN B MINOR

"They are. I don't think that's them anyways, because I didn't hear a new band member was going to join them."

"You seemed to be having a good time with Steve last night." I probe her, smiling.

"Mmm-hmm." That's her only answer on the topic. I recognize avoidance when I see it. She bumps her hip to mine. "But come on, dancer in a music video? It could change our careers. Don't tell me dancing in a music video doesn't sound appealing!"

"Hmmm…do we have to be naked? Is it an adult video?" This time my teasing her is more natural, less stiff, and my voice has less of an edge to it.

"Ha-ha, you're so funny." She scratches her nose with her index finger. "He gave me the address and the time. We would have to prepare a short choreography that would fit the theme of the song. I did find all the details on Dance World. So it has to be legit."

"What's the theme of the song?"

"Grieving, and celebrating life and moving on." She hesitates while she speaks. Because clearly, that could be the soundtrack of my life. When I don't say anything, she continues. "They're looking for one star, one dancer who is classically trained." This sounds like it could be a perfect fit. And maybe, just maybe, I could see Clément again. Do roadies go to auditions? Then it hits me. "Wait, did you tell Steve where we work?"

"Nope. I did tell him my real name though." She stares, and I feel the urge to explain myself.

"It's only the second time I used that name. And the first time was definitely needed. I didn't want to run into Irish Dude ever again. One, he was sloppy and two, he was talking about getting engaged right after. Not my plans."

Alisha shakes her head. "I don't get it. When you got back inside, you looked like you were ready to live life to the fullest."

"I was. And I did. For one night." I return her scrutinizing look. "How about Steve? When are you seeing him again?"

She tilts her head back. "At the audition, I guess. I don't know." She tries to sound like she doesn't care. But she speaks way too fast and too low. Alisha is still a novice in the art of pretending. She lights up another cigarette. I raise an eyebrow but she shrugs. "That's my last one."

"Before the next one."

"Anyways. I kind of left the club in a hurry yesterday. I don't know, I just broke up with Olivier. Everything seemed fast, way too fast." She stares at her cigarette. "I shouldn't be smoking."

"And you always say that too. While you smoke. You broke up with Olivier three months ago. If you're ready to date again, it's okay." She could call me on my BS, since I haven't dated anyone in forever.

She tenses—Alisha and I get along great and we've been confiding more and more in one another, but we both seem to have walls we like to keep around ourselves. So, I don't push her when she doesn't answer.

I tilt my head to the side. "Even if Igor doesn't suddenly decide we have to slave every night…which could very well be the case, how would we even have the time to do that?"

"Oh come on, let's try it out. You need to come with me. I can't go by myself."

"Where is it?"

"I googled the address, it's in the La Place de la République area. And it's tomorrow evening. Even if the rehearsal lasts forever…we could do it."

"We'll see. Do you know why Igor called for an early meeting?"

"Nope. To torture us, which is really his aim in life, I think." She puffs her smoke in the other direction. "I'm so sorry. Don't want to blow it in your face."

The chatter around us suddenly stops and we both turn around. Igor Baraski—our dear director—strides our way. He's still good-looking for his age, pretty much looks the same as when he was dancing as principal in the Opéra de Paris, but man he's an asshole, worse than any professors I've had at the School of Performing Arts. And even though I perfected the art of not showing I care, his remarks on how much I suck are still hard to swallow.

He crosses the courtyard without saying hello and enters the main building without looking at anyone.

LOVE IN B MINOR

He marches in followed by Audrey—the secretary of the school. She used to be a dancer too before an injury, and she decided she wanted to focus on helping new companies take off. She and Igor used to dance together at the Opéra de Paris. They brush each other and Audrey glances at him with the ghost of a smile, the kind of smile that says she knows something we don't. She looks happy, almost bursting with joy—the rumors about them being together don't sound as crazy anymore.

She hurries next to him and he slows down his pace. He leans in toward her and says something that has her tilting her head, and the connection between them is sizzling.

Did I look like that yesterday?

Alisha nudges me and I whip around her way, as if I was doing a pirouette. Staring at Audrey isn't what I'm supposed to do. I'm not supposed to check if I looked as happy yesterday. I'm supposed to forget about yesterday. A small group enters the building. Some yawn, others chitchat about the performance they saw last night at the Opéra de Paris.

Alisha dumps her cigarette in the flowerpot everyone uses as an ashtray but seems to think better of it and carries it down to the trash. "Master Igor is here. Let's go. We don't want to be late."

She links her arm with mine and together we enter the building, following the crowd into the main meeting room on the right. The company has twenty dancers and everyone is here. You'd better have a good excuse if you're ever going to not be in the building when Igor calls for a meeting.

Everybody finds a seat. Chairs screech. The whispers get louder. Igor's talking to Audrey and when she laughs, his eyes widen, his lips form a hint of a smile and he almost looks happy. But then his facial expression turns to stone and the permanent frown we've come to love and fear replaces the tiny smile.

He clears his throat. "I know you're all wondering why you're here early this morning."

"Because you like to see us suffer…" Tom, one of the principals, mutters.

But the way Igor snaps his head toward him and raises his eyebrows slowly, almost menacingly, shuts us all up. He waits for one more second, clears his throat again. It's like a redo—something he says we can never have when we're on stage. "The City of Lights Company has been having some financial issues."

Everyone startles. And someone curses in the back.

This time, Igor gives us his death glare, the one he usually only uses when we're practicing, the one that has me practicing harder than ever before, the one that brought Alisha to tears. "With the economy, and the new ballet companies surging, there's more competition. But we can do this. I know we can do it. I managed to get big journalists and donors to come to our next show, and we need to prove we have what it takes." He takes a very dramatic pause and glances at Audrey, who gives him a slight nod. I never thought Igor would need support or encouragement of any kind. Even though I should know better. "I wanted to tell you in person because there will be an article about the difficulties in the performing arts in Paris in *Le Monde* tomorrow. A preview will be online this evening. I didn't want you to hear it from someone else."

The silence in the room is oppressing. Finding a good dance company can be hard, and many of us refused positions to come here. Igor's reputation. Paris. The promises of a prestigious ballet company.

If we close, I'll need to start over.

If we close, why did I even leave New York?

I shake my head, refusing to go down that path of thinking.

Igor claps in his hands. "This may not be happy news, but I also want to make sure you understand you can make a difference. The dance company can use exposure. Positive exposure. The rumors that some dancers have fallen into drugs didn't help." He sounds mad at himself, as if it's his own personal fault that two dancers were arrested three months ago with coke. I stare at my feet, my heart beating out of my chest. He continues and I focus on his deep voice. "If you think of good ways to bring this positive exposure to the company, don't hesitate to let me know."

Alisha tentatively raises her hand. She's usually pretty shy and told me before how she never thought she could dance on stage because of her fear of speaking in public. That's why she broke down once during rehearsal when Igor poked at her weakness, yelling that she needed to get her shit together or he wouldn't put her on stage.

Igor nods her way, an eyebrow cocked to the side as if he's also surprised to hear her voice. "Would you let us audition for a role in a video?"

"You mean those rap videos with women half naked shaking their asses?" His voice is derisive.

Alisha takes a deep calming breath. "Not necessarily."

Igor raises his index finger, which could be a sign he approves or a sign he's about to tear into her idea. And I can almost feel Alisha shake next to me.

"This could be a good idea." I swear Alisha deflates and breathes more easily. "But I want to be able to approve it beforehand—your contract currently stipulates that your commitment to the City of Lights Ballet Company is exclusive unless mutually agreed." He glances at everyone in the room, throws his shoulders back, looking taller. "Listen, this article is pretty negative and even though we were able to give our side to the story, I want you to be prepared. The dancing world is a small one and people might try to contact you or recruit you. Give us a chance."

And he exits the room without taking any questions. Audrey stays behind, and her reassuring voice is almost enough to convince me that everything will be fine.

Almost.

CHAPTER 10 - LUCAS

It takes me forever to decide on what to wear for the auditions. I settle for jeans, and a comfy sweater that makes my arms look bigger, stronger. Laura, as I still call her—since I don't know what her real name might be or if she did lie about her name—said how she loved being wrapped in my arms. That may be why I'm paying extra attention today. I am usually a pro at pretending to be calm and composed, but the thought of maybe seeing her again gives me a jolt of energy.

I spent the entire day working on my new song, on the words, on the melody, spending time on the Quai de Valmy, looking at the Seine, getting inspired. It's the first time I've written a song this fast. And it feels almost perfect.

A beanie on my head and my signature sunglasses on my nose, I'm pretty sure I can stay incognito until Grégoire decides to reveal we're the band auditioning for a dancer. The doorman opens the door of the five-star hotel for me. The lobby is full of light and already crowded. A few journalists mingle with the dancers. Grégoire did say this audition was going to be a big marketing event. Steve told me this morning the buzz was all about discovering which band had organized this audition. And I'm sure Grégoire will "leak" the story to the press, making it seem like this wasn't all planned from the beginning. Grégoire may be good at managing, but I disagree with a lot of his techniques. Benji did too. I remember them arguing to no end, about how Grégoire wanted Benji to date some girl from his old neighborhood to push a new demographics of fans. However, when Benji's grandmother was diagnosed with Alzheimer's, Grégoire did find her the best care possible.

LOVE IN B MINOR

I can't think about that now. I can't think about
Benji.

A lot of dancers showed up. I stretch my neck to
see if I find *her*. But no luck and I can't attract the
attention.

I wave at the receptionist in the entrance.
Grégoire told me I could reach the audition room by
walking through the restaurant and turning left.

Our security guards let me in. Steve and Dimitri
are sitting together, laughing loudly. And there's a
woman who waves at me. Probably the assistant of the
director who will shoot the music video. Grégoire
stands by the door as if he's been waiting for me.
"We're starting in ten minutes," Grégoire informs me,
emphasizing the "ten minutes" as if he thinks I can't
remember time.

Dimitri stretches and yawns loudly. "I don't
understand why we all have to be here."

"Good question," I reply, staring at Grégoire.
I've got a lingering feeling the reason he absolutely
wanted all of us to be there was because he planned
something big for the band. Something bigger than just

revealing which band is casting for a dancer. Something I probably won't like. But he's good at pretending. And he's good at asking others to pretend too. He wanted Benji to pretend to fall in love. He wanted Benji to pretend he didn't have a drug problem. He wanted Benji to pretend to be someone else. Benji never managed to do that: to steel himself against the truth and against the pain.

Anger simmers at the surface. Grégoire and I have been arguing a lot since Benji died; I almost punched him once, but I've promised to rein my rage in. There's no way to break our contract with him without losing everything we all worked so hard for, and I can't forget the early days, when Grégoire fought for us, fought to put us on a map, was there for us. Fame does change people. Fame can show the ugly side of people.

I need to take a breather. "I'll be right back." I turn to Steve and Dimitri. Both of them look pretty aloof, as if my mood swings aren't new.

Grégoire nods but frowns. "Don't be late."

LOVE IN B MINOR

"I won't." I exit the same way I came in, but instead of walking back into the restaurant, I continue down the hallway.

And then I freeze.

Because in front of me, wearing a small skirt and an apologetic smile, stands the one person I never thought I would see again.

Especially not here.

CHAPTER 11 - JEN

"I didn't think so many girls would be here!" I whisper to Alisha, who is staring straight ahead, her posture way too stiff. The smell of coffee during the evening has become familiar to me in Paris. Coffee in the morning, after lunch, midafternoon, sometimes after dinner. And the coffee is strong. But I've become addicted. People in the hotel restaurant are having an early dinner—most restaurants seem to be full around seven or eight in the evening usually, and it's only 6:30 p.m.

The dozens of girls ahead of us in the line should have warned us that this audition was going to be packed, but I didn't expect to see at least fifty girls already waiting in the lobby.

"Me neither. Maybe we should turn back," she says, and there's a note of resignation in her voice. Something I can't accept from her, because she's an amazing dancer and she's dedicated and the sweetest. She reminds me of my friend Emilia—except Emilia didn't want to dance. I saw it almost right away, and I was right. A tinge of nostalgia pinches my heart thinking about Emilia…how we became friends. Unlikely friends, since I did at one point think her now-boyfriend and I had a chance.

"What do you think? Let's go home?" Alisha steps back and almost runs into me.

"I think we should go for it. We've got our numbers." I point to the folder we received when signing up. "And we have a room to warm up in. Plus, you heard Igor…we could help the company."

"You hate Igor."

"I don't hate him. I think he's a pompous ass who really enjoys looking at himself in the mirror, but he's talented and I believe in the company." And I don't want to think I left New York for nothing. That I wasn't there for my sister when she died for no reason at all. I can feel the anger, the despair simmering. Before I would have pushed Alisha away, but I promised my sister—Mia—that I would try to be better.

That I would try to love and be strong and live my dreams. Because she couldn't.

"Jen, you need to promise me," Mia—my six-year-old sister—tells me. She sounds so much older. Her face has more color than the weeks before and her voice is stronger. The new treatment they started seems promising—even if it is just buying her time, they're talking about at least one year. And I want to spend this year with her. But she cried when I told her I was going to stay with her.

We're in her hospital room, surrounded by teddy bears and her favorite superhero figures. She's wearing her superwoman costume and I wish—yet again—that some superhuman force could help her, save her, eradicate the cancer.

LOVE IN B MINOR

"I don't want you to stay. I don't want to see you if you stay," she growls. "You're going to be back in a month for two weeks and I'll be here."

"I want to stay." The ballet company that wants to hire me gave me an extension, but they said they can't keep my spot longer than October. And October is in two days.

"Jen. You've got to promise me three things. And you got to pinky swear," she says.

"Anything," I reply and hold out my pinky, linking it with hers. She's so cold. So cold. I struggle to keep my tears inside. Everyone thinks I'm such a stuck-up bitch, but they don't know it's my way of stopping the pain. My sister knows me. She knows who I truly am, and even though I want to hope that they'll find a cure, I know it's unlikely.

"You have to find someone who makes you happy." She tilts her chin to the books sprawled on the floor. "Like in the fairy tales Mom reads to me."

My fairy-tale ending would be that she enters remission. I stopped believing in fairy tales a long time ago.

"I can't control that." I try to laugh but the sound is pitiful.

"Yes, you can." She sounds so serious, but then a real smile breaks on her face and my heart melts. *"You're so nice. And you're so pretty. And I love you. Everyone should love you too."* I'm not half as nice as she thinks I am. I didn't get the reputation I have for nothing. She should be the one experiencing the world, discovering who she is, falling in love.

"Hmm." That's the only answer I can give her.

"Promise me you're going to go to Paris."

I shake my head. *"I can't go to Paris. I would need to be there in two days at the latest."* The company has done all the paperwork for me and technically I could go, but I don't want to. I want to, but I don't want to.

She bores her eyes into mine. *"Promise me you're going to go to Paris."* She holds our fingers higher up. *"You're pinky swearing. You can't take it back."* She wheezes and I'm about to call her nurse, when she continues. *"They already gave you an extension because of me. I heard Mom and Dad talk about it. And I'm better."* Her voice wavers. *"Please, go. For me."*

And I went. And she died while I was gone. I don't want to think about it.

Alisha and I make our way through the crowd of dancers who eye us up and down, but I give as good as I get. They don't scare me. They should be worried about us. We come from one of the best—even though apparently not financially sound—companies in the world. That and I'm an amazing dancer.

I stop in front of a girl who seems a bit less judgmental: "Have you heard which band is auditioning?"

"Well, some thought it could a French band or singer, but I don't think so. Someone else brought up Villain Complex, but why would they be in France to find someone to dance in their videos? There are rumors that it could be Dire Blue."

"Who are they?"

Her eyes widen and her laugh is way too loud—a bunch of people turn to us. I keep my head high. Not my fault I have no time whatsoever to listen to music.

I'm into Netflix and podcasts. When I take a shower, I listen to the first season of *Serial*—that's the only time I have to myself.

"Thanks." I smile as widely as I can to show her that I really don't care about what she thinks.

Which I don't.

Alisha pushes the door to the rehearsing room. Three other girls are in there, but they completely ignore us. "I wish we could google those bands. I can't believe they took all of our stuff at the entrance."

"I guess that was their point though. Keep the element of surprise. Or whatever." I take off my sweater and stretch down to the floor. My energy is all over the place. Being nervous or anxious before a performance is perfectly normal, but that's not what I'm feeling right now. It's more complicated.

I touch my toes and then throw my arm over my head. Alisha's in the zone. Her eyes don't dart all over the place like mine. There's a paint crack underneath the large window on the right and the décor's a bit too in-my-face for my taste. The golden panels, the old coffee table that looks like it should be in a historic film.

Concentrate, Jen. Concentrate.

I close my eyes. Big mistake. The smell in the room reminds me of the hospital my sister stayed in. I think it's the product they used on the window.

Sadness replaces the anticipation. I'm back in New York for one of the performances I've done for Mia and her friends at the hospital before we heard she qualified for that new treatment, the new treatment that was supposed to save her time, the new treatment we had put all of our hopes on. The new treatment that failed.

"Again!" Mia claps her hands. "Do it again!" Her voice is frail but her smile still shines. The other kids in the community room join her pleas, and I bow into a deep reverence.

I nod toward the nurse and she puts the music to the beginning again. One step to the right, one step to the left and a pirouette. Even though it appears that I'm lost in the music and the movement, I'm aware of everything: the strong hospital smell, the tubes and

machines surrounding the children, the way one mom wipes away her tears, hiding so her kid doesn't see her. I try to smile her way, a smile to tell her I understand and that I'm there for her, I want to be there for all of them. One way or another.

My sister is dying and there's nothing I can do. Nothing. Nothing, except not show her how destroyed I am to see her slip away. I can't show her how much I want to hold on to her and never let her go. The sadness lodges itself in my throat, hard and unforgivable.

I raise my arms above my head. My sister imitates me and again, I'm amazed by how strong, how courageous the children are. Much more than me.

I'm almost out of breath by the time the next song stops. The kids clap one more time.

"Okay, time to go back to your rooms," one of the nurses says in a warm voice. Mia calls my name softly.

"You were amazing."

"Remember, one day, you'll be on stage with me."

LOVE IN B MINOR

"I don't think so." Her skin is much paler than yesterday. How is that even possible? I want to scream but I keep my fake smile in place.

"You'll be in a tutu and you'll do a pirouette."

"I love you." She glances down at her feet and then stares into my eyes. Her beautiful dark eyes seem tormented. I gently take her hand in mine. And her voice breaks. "I'm going to die."

I touch my nose and open my eyes, blinking rapidly to not cry here and now. It took me so long to build up that façade, but one little memory and it crumbles.

"I need to go to the bathroom," I mumble. I don't really need to go to the bathroom, but I need to get out of this room before I break down

Alisha stops in her movements. "You're okay?"

"Why wouldn't I be?" My tone is curt but it's so much easier to be angry than to be sad. I dig my fingers into the palms of my hand, one at a time, reminding myself of the promise I gave Mia. I don't know if my six-year-old sister knew how much what she asked would resonate with me. "I'm sorry. I'm fine." I head out of the rehearsal room, but I don't want to go through the lines of dancers. My game face isn't on. They'll see the weakness and during an audition like this, I need to come out on top. Because that's what I do. I work hard. I sacrifice everything and dancing is the only thing that makes me forget, makes me happy.

I turn to the hallway to the right.

The crowd dims and there's a sign for the bathrooms. One more right.

At first my brain can't register.

The tall frame. The dark brownish hair. The deep voice.

"I should go. You and I are over and you know it," he says, and there's so much sadness in that last word. He hasn't noticed me yet. He's wearing jeans and a dark burgundy sweatshirt. And I can picture him lying on his bed, taking his clothes off, holding me— his fingers trailing down my back.

Is it me or did someone crank up the temperature in here? I knew I might find him here, since he works for Steve's band, but his presence still takes me by surprise.

LOVE IN B MINOR

My heart leaps into a frantic grand jeté.

My lips go on automatic mode and stretch into a happy smile. And then I see the girl wrapping her arms around him, the way he rests his head on top of hers like it's familiar, full of feelings, real.

It's the girl from the picture. Translucent skin, gorgeous red hair.

My heart misses its landing and crashes into the bottom of my chest.

The hope that was floating in tiny bubbles deep in my stomach, that I was trying to ignore, that I was pushing away, explodes.

What goes around comes around.

They still haven't seen me. And I am tempted to run away from everything, but I'm a professional. So what if I feel like a horde of backup dancers got up and danced the *Swan Lake* on my body? I'm the queen of dealing with the awkwardness, with the hurt, with the mistakes. Clément was a one-night stand.

Nothing more.

CHAPTER 12 - LUCAS

"You know how sorry I am." Olivia's voice is sweet and sugary. Her voice is a lie that hits me in the guts. She still looks the same. The same red hair that appears to be on fire. The same smile that captured my heart once. The same full lips I kissed so many times.

I unwrap her arms from my neck and step back. Seeing her is overwhelming, is a mix of emotions I wasn't prepared to deal with. Not today.

Even though she betrayed me and lied to me, my ex Olivia was also the one who was by my side when Benji died. She held my hand at the funeral. She gave me space and hugged me when I needed it. She was there at the beginning, when we weren't famous or rich yet.

Olivia tilts her head to the side, twirls a strand of hair around her finger. Playing innocent, she was always so good at playing innocent.

"I miss you," she whispers, batting her eyelashes in that way she always had. And maybe she does. And maybe I miss the idea of her, but I don't miss her. She hurt me too much. Shit, she used me.

"I don't know what you're playing, but I'm not playing with you."

"I'll change your mind. Come on, Lucas, don't you remember how we were?"

"You mean the day you sold pictures of us to make sure you stayed in the news. Without asking me first?" I want to punch the wall but instead I curl my hands into fists. I still don't understand it.

"I apologized. And come on, Lucas, you know we're good together. And that song you wrote, the one for the music video, you know it was for me."

My laugh is bitter. The song I wrote for the music video is about Benji. I wrote it six weeks after his death and before yesterday, it was the last song I could bring myself to write. She can't be serious if she thinks it's about her. She always thought it was always about her.

She takes one tiny step forward. "I have to go. I'll see you inside."

She's a good singer, but she's not a classically trained ballet dancer, and she's not right for the part. "Are you auditioning?"

"Of course not. You know my dancing is good but not that good." And for a second, when she glances my way with so much mischief into her eyes, I remember the fifteen-year-old she was, how she always found a way to make me smile. She bites her lip, glances down before meeting my eyes again. She always did that when she knew I wasn't going to agree with something: like when I didn't agree to go on some reality TV show and she got mad, or when I refused to do a show three days after Benji died and she left the band because she didn't understand why I wanted to take a break from music, or when I broke up with her after she gave the journalists pictures of us in Corsica three weeks after Benji passed away.

At least she had the decency to tell me about the pictures, about using my name to get a meeting with a top producer when she went solo. She always told me after the fact, even when I disagreed with her. Almost always. There was one time she didn't and created a whole mess.

"Olivia?" I press her.

"You're not going to be happy. But you have to listen to me until the end."

I cross my arms over my chest in a move she used to say was one more way for me to keep her at a distance. "Apparently, Grégoire wants to try to bring in a female part for the song you wrote. He said it was a song about how hard it was to move on. He said it's a song that means a lot to me too."

"What?" My voice rises—I can't help it. I can't have heard this clearly. Obviously, I'm imagining things. Not on that song. Not on the song about Benji. That song has nothing to do with her, despite what

Grégoire said. Grégoire has always been mesmerized by her. Always.

"He asked me to come today so I can watch the auditions, spend time with you guys and maybe we could all talk after."

"No."

"Come on, Lucas. I'm not scheming anything. I'm not doing anything wrong. Your manager asked me to pass by. And I'm so happy to see you but I know you don't trust me and I thought maybe like this, we can put the past behind us." She bites the skin of her index finger. I don't think she realizes she's doing it. "It's not easy right now. I'm not doing so well. And I need a push."

"Like you did when you went behind my back and talked about me? Like you did when you lied to people saying I proposed?" I breathe out, calming myself. "I had to call my mom and tell her it wasn't true. It created a shitstorm when we issued a denial and the groupies blamed it on my parents, who would have said they didn't want me to marry so young. I know you love the attention, but they didn't. They got hate messages, and they were followed for weeks afterwards not only by paparazzi, but by crazy fans who wanted to convince them that they were wrong." My voice rises. "I always told you to leave my family out of the spotlight. You knew how much that meant to me and you didn't care."

"But that's not true. I never went to the press with that story. I would have told you! Marie and I were having a drink on the terrace of a bar and I was telling her how I thought we weren't too young to get married, how if you would propose I wouldn't say no. That part is true but not the rest."

I clench my fists. "Bullshit. Marie doesn't remember that discussion."

She rolls her eyes and her voice rises. "Whatever, you can believe what you want. Let's face it, Lucas. The reason you pushed me away was because of Benji, not anything you've mentioned."

"Do not talk about Benji." My tone is on the edge, ready to fall into a canyon of anger and despair. There's nothing for us to discuss now. Nothing left but messy feelings and a past we can never touch again.

"Lucas, please."

Tears fill her eyes as if I hurt her. "You know how sorry I am. You know how much I miss him too. You know I really tried—"

I cut off her apologies. Almost afraid of what she's going to say. "I don't want to hear it, not now."

She straightens, passes her fingers through her hair. "All I'm asking for is a chance… You know how much my career means to me. And I feel like I'm drowning."

"As manager, Grégoire can do a lot of things. He can let you audition for example and he can find some loophole in the band's contract that forces us to sing with you. Not much I can say about that, but I'm asking you to not do it. Not for this song."

"I need to, Lucas. I need the money and I need the exposure."

I shake my head. "Don't fuck it up then."

And I walk away.

Because walking away is easier than facing the truth.

CHAPTER 13 - JEN

The walk back to the room where Alisha's still rehearsing is almost surreal and definitely painful. Painful because I've been there.

I've done that.

The girl from the picture, the one who was hugging him so tightly, she clearly means something to him, even if I don't think they're together right now. I'm not getting in the middle of a relationship I don't understand. My heart got stomped on when I tried that in New York. Back then, I thought…I don't know what I thought, except Nick and I had so much in common and he always looked at me in a certain way. Nick was the star student of the School of Performing Arts, like me. He was dedicated, like me. He made it seem like he cared and I held on to that.

But soon enough it was clear I didn't belong with him.

I can't go through this again. I'm still working on so many issues and there's the company and there are my parents who threw themselves in their work to forget the death of my little sister, and at the same time forgot about me.

I purse my lips, ignoring how loud my heart is beating, how fast my mind is racing.

I need to concentrate on the here and now. Otherwise, I can forget everything, pack my bags and take the next plane home.

And then what? I go home and everything I fought for, everything I missed, every mistake I've made has been for nothing.

I'm tempted to kick the wall or to scream, but I'm pretty sure that could get me kicked out of the auditions.

LOVE IN B MINOR

I need to relax my face into something that doesn't resemble a scowl. Scowling can work in certain situations—but an audition isn't usually the place to look like you're about to explode any second.

I inhale and exhale slowly and push open the door to the rehearsal room. The light is dimmer and Alisha is the only one left in there. She's stretching on the floor. Her legs in a split, she pushes her body on her front leg.

She shrieks when I enter and then giggles. "You scared the crap out of me."

I turn on the lights. The darkness is almost complete outside and the small windows don't help much. "Sorry, didn't mean to startle you." My voice is too robotic.

"Are you okay?" Alisha must have picked up on it. She tilts her head slightly to the side as if she can figure out what's wrong with me.

"I'm okay." I chew on my upper lip and then stop. It's one of my tells that I'm really stressed. That and getting stomachaches. And man, my stomach hurts right now. "A tad worried. The girls here seem to be good. I think Erin and Nadia are here from our ballet company."

"Really?" Erin is the newest member of the company, and Nadia is amazing. She quit the Opéra de Paris when Igor opened his own ballet company, and she's been a star in the two previous shows.

"It makes sense. If the auditions are as big as Steve said on Saturday night and now that we have Igor's approval, it does make a lot of sense." She shrugs. "We just have to be better than everyone else." She stands up and grabs her folder, bringing it tightly to her chest as if it can shield her from stage fright. "Are you ready?"

"As ready as I'll be." I want to tell her about Clément, about seeing him here, about seeing him fighting with that other girl, about my string of bad luck when it comes to boys. Granted, sometimes it may not have been bad luck, but bad timing or bad choices. Nick wasn't the first one I tried to hold on to, and at least Nick was a nice guy. Not like others.

But again, I can't really blame them.

LOVE IN B MINOR

Either I didn't give them a chance or I tried too hard.

With Clément, even if it was only one night, I felt like myself. And it wasn't as scary as I thought it would be.

We take a spot in the hallway, ignoring the stares. "Erin is over there," I whisper, but Alisha isn't as discreet. "Hey, Erin!" she calls, and Erin skips to us with a big smile on her face like she's relieved to see us here. She seems pretty nice. I haven't seen her sabotage anybody, but that could be a skill she's only learning. Most of the girls at the company are ruthless.

"Hi!" Her voice is soothing. "I don't know what the heck I'm doing here." Her British accent gets stronger with each word. "Since Igor agreed we could audition outside of the company, my sister who follows everything music-related told me about this one. I thought why not…but I'm so not ready. What if they're super famous? I might freeze."

"You won't." My voice could be warmer, but I'm being pragmatic because the likelihood of her freezing is actually very low. To make it to this stage, she had to audition a thousand times, she had to perform in different places, she probably had to act in a certain way even when she felt sick to her stomach or when she didn't want to move at all.

"Eight hundred and eight," a tiny woman with the most piercings I've ever seen calls, and Erin glances from me to Alisha.

"That's me." She stares at the number in her hand, but doesn't move.

"Eight hundred and eight!"

"You can do it." Alisha pushes her forward.

I take one tiny step to Erin, whose eyes are still full of fear. "You danced every single day—rain, shine, holidays, sickness. Your feet bled, you cried, you probably even screamed. You put yourself in ice baths that didn't help. No matter who is inside, what band it is, you can show them a thing or two about dedication."

She nods and slowly moves forward without a word. But at least her head is high.

Alisha turns and nudges me. "You're a pretty good motivational speaker."

LOVE IN B MINOR

"Erin's working hard. She's always getting yelled at by Igor, but she's trying and she's good and she wants it."

"Who isn't getting yelled at by Igor?"

"You have a point." I half smile before remembering that I may see Clément in that room. Do roadies stay during auditions?

I close my eyes. I need to concentrate.

But apparently, Alisha needs to talk. "What was your best performance ever?"

I could lie and say it was my last showcase at the School. I could lie and pretend my best performance was my happiest one. I could lie and say it was the one that opened doors for me.

But I won't lie.

Talking about Mia is keeping her alive, and even though talking about her also tightens my chest to the point where I can't breathe, telling the truth right now is more important than protecting myself.

"When my sister was at the hospital, I used to go all dressed up with a tutu and dramatic makeup and dance for her and the other kids. When I left for Paris, they thought she was doing a bit better, that they had found a new drug that would help her live longer. So my last performance there was the morning before my plane took off. I danced for her and with her and with her friends and she was laughing. She was smiling. It was the last time I saw her."

I need to fight away the tears, and I'm not even sure Alisha can hear the last words I say.

A girl walks past us, shooting us death glares. "They're already crying. Must be that article in *Le Monde*. Clearly, Igor should have thought twice about leaving the Opéra de Paris." She enunciates each word slowly and loudly enough for me to hear but low enough so the guards at the entrance don't.

I take a deep breath. If my voice breaks it won't be as efficient. Alisha gasps but doesn't say a word. I step up to the ballerina turned mean girl. "My little sister died three months and a half ago. That's why I was crying. And trust me, in her entire six years on this Earth, she showed more grace than you ever will. And you're a dancer."

LOVE IN B MINOR

I don't bother to check her reaction. Or to answer to her mumbled apologies.

Alisha squeezes my hand.

The tiny woman with the piercings comes back out. "Number eight hundred and nine." That's Alisha.

Her body stiffens but I squeeze her hand back. "You can do this."

She throws her shoulders back and glides to the door like she owns it. The girls behind me now whisper about the latest gossip. Another one mentions the newspaper article and even though she's more discreet about it, it still stings. "Those poor dancers. Clearly, they should have chosen another company. I guess the glitz and promise of quick fame was enough for them."

I guess she didn't hear me put the other one back in her place. She doesn't know me. "I guess some dancers have too much time on their hands." I step to her and eye her up and down. "You're from the Lyon Ballet Company, right?"

Her eyes widen. People have a tendency to become much quieter if you actually call them on their bullshit. "I believe you got that spot because I turned them down. They tried to convince me for days."

And I whip my head back away from her. Her friend is consoling her. Telling her I clearly have a problem. Yes, I do. Actually, I have way more than one. But right now, her not owing up to her issues is my issue. Because I know those girls. I caught myself once or twice being one of those girls. And I didn't like what I was seeing.

I focus back on myself. I shouldn't let all of them derail me. I've got enough on my plate.

The choreography I prepared isn't too difficult, but I thought for a dancer in a music video, I should focus more on something that can transcend: a few visual movements that may look complicated, and trying as much as possible to convey emotions.

And after talking about Mia, my emotions are all over the place.

Erin took about five minutes. They make all girls exit via a different exit. To not spoil the surprise, I guess. It's already been ten minutes and they still haven't called my name. Alisha must be doing well.

LOVE IN B MINOR

Competition is cutthroat in this world, but I'd rather lose to the best than not show up. Some dancers may be better than me, but if they don't have the passion for it, then it won't work for them. That was the case for my friend, Emilia.

Dancing is my passion and it's my career and it's what keeps me together.

"Number eight hundred ten!" The tiny woman is back. And that's my number.

I rub my hands and then clench them into fists. Only one second to put on my happy and confident face.

I take a deep breath and turn around to the girl who tried to derail me earlier. "May the best ballerina get the role."

She purses her lips, but I don't care. I enter the audition room.

The woman motions for me to stand in the middle of the room. I don't look at anybody—even though I'm dying to check if Clément is there.

It resembles other audition rooms: the piano standing in the corner, the smell of anticipation. It's a mix of deodorant and perfume and tears. Because I know for sure at least one person cried in this room today. I cried once during an audition and only once. That was the year I auditioned for the School of Performing Arts, and I wasn't made of steel yet. I messed up one step and thought I had missed my chance. Svetlana—my favorite teacher there—came to talk to me after the audition, telling me I had talent and they saw it. I only needed to see it too.

Clément is here. My heart pounds. He's at the table. The table in the middle with the people who will watch and judge every single movement. He stares at me with his mouth gaping open. Our eyes collide and I'm the one to look away. Because I shouldn't feel this happy, this drawn to him.

Steve waves at me with a warm smile, but he doesn't say a word.

"Laura?" Clément's voice almost does me in. My feet itch to run away, but I use the adrenaline slamming into my veins to focus on what I need to do. I smile my sweetest smile, which also happens to be my fakest smile.

LOVE IN B MINOR

I inhale deeply, step forward with my resume, my headshot, my paperwork. We had to sign a Non-Disclosure Agreement.

Why is he sitting at the table? If he's a roadie, shouldn't he be doing roadie things, whatever those are?

And she's here too. Can this day get any worse? At least she's not sitting next to him. She's on the other side of the table and she's staring me down. She's staring at me like she already hates me.

The older man with grayish temples taps his fingers on the table like my mere presence annoys him.

"Welcome," he says with a voice that says I'm not welcome at all. "I'm Grégoire Sarant—I'm the manager of the band." He doesn't bother to introduce anyone else. "The name of her file says Jennifer. Jennifer Harrison." His eyes roam all over my body and his index finger now touches his upper lip. I stay silent even though I have at least one thousand questions. He opens his mouth, closes it and then opens it again. "Wait, that's the girl who was outside the club, the girl you went to look for?"

I remember him. Before Clément came to help me, he was walking by and turned away. "And you're the guy who didn't help when he saw that stupid meathead annoying me."

"You seemed to have the situation under control."

"Checking in wouldn't have hurt." And that's not the way I'm going to get this part.

Clément turns to Grégoire. "You saw her with the guy who tried to mug her and you didn't do anything?" He sounds more than pissed, he sounds outraged.

"I didn't know he was mugging her, and that's not the point."

Clément takes a deep breath and rubs the back of his neck, trying to calm down, and I wish I could go up to him and talk to him but I stay put.

He clears his throat. And it's like he can't stop looking at me. And there's so much confusion on his face, probably reflecting mine. "So, Jennifer."

"Jen. You can call me Jen."

"I'm Lucas Wills. Lucas Clément Wills."

LOVE IN B MINOR

I frown slightly. I know that name. I've heard that name.

"She probably knows who you are. Probably planned this whole thing." The guy next to Lucas is getting on my last nerve, and staying stoic is starting to be too hard. Lucas, it sounds good. He looks like a Lucas. I shake my head slightly.

The girl from the picture leans forward. "Clearly, they slept together, let's move on." Her tone is dismissive but there's pain in her eyes.

"Olivia." Lucas' tone is a warning and she doesn't say another word.

Talk about awkward.

"I'm here for the audition. Nothing more." And I cringe at the sound of my voice. I sound annoyed and bitchy and like I don't give a care in the world.

Lucas sits back, and the way he crosses his arms is a stark reminder of the way he crossed his arms when I first asked him to bake cookies.

"Well, you're here," he says. "So let's watch you dance." It's like he doesn't believe in my ability to impress them, or maybe he doesn't believe me. Like me lying about my name was such a big deal. He lied too....

Lucas Wills—I can't believe I didn't recognize him. Granted, I only know his songs and not his face, but come on…

"I'm ready."

And when the music starts, Lucas becomes my anchor point. He's the one I look at, when I do pirouette after pirouette. The melody is sad, so sad. And it reminds me of everything I've lost, of all the heartache and the tears.

I feel every movement, every arch of my arm, every jump.

I feel the music resonate within me.

I feel alive.

His face doesn't tell me anything. I'm not sure if he's pissed or happy to see me. I shouldn't even care. I shouldn't want to reach out and touch his face, snuggle up to him, talk to him, make him laugh.

When the music stops, I'm out of breath. I'm waiting for a reaction. Any. The guys all look at Lucas, but the girl—Olivia—is staring at me. And she doesn't look like we're going to be BFFs anytime soon.

Grégoire—the manager—opens his mouth but Lucas touches his shoulder, stopping him from saying anything.

Lucas stands up and he owns the room. I'm not sure if it's his confident posture, or his strong jaw, or simply the fact that he's there, entirely there.

He strides to the piano.

"What are you doing?" his manager asks him. And he doesn't sound pleased. The other guys at the table seem pretty chill. Steve even discreetly gives me a thumbs-up.

"I want to see if she can improvise to the song I wrote two nights ago."

My eyes widen and my hand rubs the back of my neck. I rise on my toes, stretch, then lower again. A mechanism to stop my heart from beating too fast.

He walks by me, almost touching me, and warmth spreads within me. He's got too much of a pull on me.

I manage to swallow my nervousness and my voice almost sounds calm when I reply. "Sure."

"I'll play the melody first so you can get an idea of the tempo and then I'll sing with it."

His manager stands up, sighing loudly—the same way my parents did when they thought I was being a spoiled brat. "No one else had to do that."

"And?" Lucas sounds annoyed, but like he's trying to reign himself in.

"It's not fair."

"I'll still give a fair chance to everyone who has auditioned and everyone who will audition."

"Every single one of them? And will you think about doing what's best for the band?" His manager enunciates each word slowly, and they glare at each other. There's some intense eye battle going on there.

Lucas sighs, giving in, it seems, to whatever silent argument they were having. "I'll give a fair chance to every single one of them, and yes, I will think about what's best for the band." That seems to calm his manager down. He sits back down and takes out his phone, dismissing Lucas, dismissing us and whatever is about to happen.

Lucas' fingers touch the keys of the piano and he looks more like the guy I spent time with. Why does it feel like it's only the two of us in the audition room?

"Are you ready?" He's staring right at me and then his gaze drops to my lips. "Are you sure you want to do this?"

I chuckle. He knows exactly what he's doing by asking me this. Those were his exact words before…before we tumbled into bed.

I was sure then. But now? Standing in this room, looking at him, being so close to him? Wondering what his reasons for lying were?

I've never felt so exposed, so vulnerable, less sure in my entire life.

Lucas Wills could make my career.

But…he could also break my heart.

CHAPTER 14 - LUCAS

She's feeling the same way I am—I could see it in the way her breath hitched when I walked past her, in the way she licked her lower lip without even realizing it. She did that right before I kissed her for the first time. I shouldn't be thinking about that. If she ends up getting the role—and let's face it, she's the best so far—I will need to stay away from her. I can't get involved with someone I work with again.

When the band became famous, it all went to shit. She felt the pressure, the competition, the need to be first. All those demands she had about us, about pushing us into the media while all I wanted was to lie low and do music. She used me and the band to get where she wanted. But I guess the destination wasn't worth it if she's crawling back to sing with us.

And now Grégoire wants us to work together again? I'd tell him off but a part of me knows he's right.

I glance up at Jen from the piano. Jen…I wish I could have a redo of two nights ago, and have her whisper my real name, call her real name as my lips discover her entire body.

Those thoughts are making my jeans very uncomfortable. And I can't help but tease her, make her remember like I am right now.

"Are you ready?" Her eyes widen oh so slightly. It's like she knows exactly where I'm going with this. I almost wink at her, but I restrain myself. I wouldn't hear the end of it. Which let's face it, I don't give a fuck about, but she wouldn't hear the end of it either and that I care about. I barely know her but I have this need to protect her, to help her, to be by her side. And people would think she got the role because of what happened between us. I continue to look at her.

"Are you sure you want to do this?" My voice drops a little. Huskier.

Her cheeks blush and I am giving myself an internal high five.

"I am not only sure I want to do this, I'm going to explode if we don't do it right now," she whispers. I'm pretty sure I'm the only one who hears the words, and I have to clear my throat and turn to the piano to avoid rushing to her and kissing her in front of everyone.

I had been wanting to see her again.

I had been searching for her.

And now that she's standing so near to me, there's nothing I can do.

But I do want her to hear the song she inspired. I want to see her dance to it. I want to see the look on her face when she hears the words.

CHAPTER 15 - JEN

"Are you okay, bro?" Steve, who sat on the right of Lucas, asks him. And Lucas nods. I'm sure I'm gloating but two can play this game.

"Great."

His fingers are back on the keys. And then he starts playing. And I forget I'm supposed to come up with an improvisation because the melody is heart-wrenching and hopeful all at once and it's exactly how I've been feeling these past months—like a part of me is lost, but I hope that one day I'll feel whole again.

I'm pretty sure my mouth gapes open and I must look like all his groupies. But instead of saying anything, I close my eyes, forget where I am and simply dance. He starts from the beginning again—still without any words. It's like he can read me.

I raise my arms above my head.

Glide to the side in a *pas chassé* and then turn with my left leg in an *arabesque*. I imagine him dancing with me. I imagine seeing my sister again and telling her everything I wish I could have said. I imagine living life to the fullest, risking everything, including my heart.

I jump into a *grand jeté.*

The room is mine, the music invades me and my movements. I feel it, all of it.

When the music stops, Steve claps his hands. "Wow, that was awesome!" Even their manager looks a bit mollified. He actually let go of his phone. Olivia—however—purses her lips and she glances from me to Lucas.

I keep my eyes trained on them, because I can't bring myself to look at him. What if he hated it? What if he didn't think I portrayed his melody like he thought it should be? Being an artist, I understand how those notes are a part of himself.

His voice is clouded with something I can't clearly point my finger on. "Let's do it again. This time with the lyrics."

I nod.

"No one has heard it yet," he says. "Jen?" He calls my name and I can't keep on ignoring him without looking rude. I turn to him, and my heart skips a beat.

I gulp. Because he's looking at me the same way he did that night. Like I'm the only one who understands him, the only one who can make him laugh, the only one.

This time, when his fingers touch the keys, I don't look away. I don't close my eyes.

But when he starts singing, I freeze.

Because those words? Those words are about us.

CHAPTER 16 - LUCAS

Even Grégoire seems impressed. Olivia looks stricken and for a split second, I feel sorry for her…she was always so good at making me feel sorry for her. But the moment passes and I focus on Jen. Only on her.

The way she dances…it's everything I had hoped for when I saw her in the room. And my heart bursts with pride for her, even though a part of me, that nasty voice that doubts people don't have any ulterior motives, does wonder if maybe she didn't orchestrate this entire thing: the meeting, the evening…the night.

LOVE IN B MINOR

I can't think about that now. The energy running through my body begs to be released and the adrenaline drums all the way to my fingertips. No one has ever heard that song. That song I composed the morning after she tiptoed outside of my apartment and disappeared from my life like she was only a figment of my imagination.

What happened to the happily ever after of our childhood fairy tales.

What happened to our dreams?

Life was passing me by. Simply going through the motions.

Could not believe in anything, not in them and definitely not in me.

People smiling about everything, about nothing and I stay empty,

Refusing to feel any emotions.

Too hard. Too painful. Too damn heartbreaking.

You found me and healed me. Only one night of your magic.

Only night of your touch and I can breathe again. I can believe again.

Even though the night ended. Even though you left me stranded.

You showed me that feeling is everything.

You're the girl who got away.
The girl who got away.
The one-night stand who got away.
Your touch and your whispers.
Your skin against mine. I remember everything.

I see her stiffen for only a second. She stops mid-movement, but then she continues and seeing her dancing to my words, to those words that are all about her, it's everything I didn't know I wanted.

Now if only I could tell the nasty voice in my head that's wondering if she's used me to shut the fuck up.

CHAPTER 17 - JEN

Dancing to those words is exciting and excruciating. Exciting because if he wrote those words, he must mean them, right?

Excruciating because what am I going to do? Sleeping with the guy who might be your boss is usually frowned upon. And I've seen that girl—Olivia—blinking tears away.

Plus, being in a relationship would mean opening up, and being myself, and that I can't do.

Being in France means reinventing myself. When I left the city, I promised myself I'd leave my past in the past. And certain things are definitely better left in the past. Plus, come on, the fiasco with Nick taught me that I can become too attached, too certain about something. And then crashing down hurts like hell.

I turn to the right, do a small *pas chassé* before arching my back.

His voice goes back to the main chorus and it's like he's near me, like he's whispering those words into my ear.

My heart beats faster and faster, while my movements become even more fluid, even fuller of meaning.

You're the girl who got away.
The girl who got away.
The one-night stand who got away.
Your touch and your whispers.
Your skin against mine. I remember everything.
We said no promises. No fake tomorrows. Just one night.

LOVE IN B MINOR

Just one night isn't enough, it has to be the beginning.

Of something more.

My feet take me on a slow spin, and when the music stops, part of me stays with it. Lucas is about to say something. He has to say something.

He stands up and the way he smiles, the way he moves is everything I want to know. He meant every word.

But his manager cuts him off. "This was lovely. We will call you to let you know our decision."

And wow, that was dry and cold and pretty much put me back in my place. I go to gather my clothes and my bag. "Thank you for your time."

I'm tempted to tell Lucas I want to see him again. Clearly, the manager isn't a fan of mine, and I probably won't get the part if he has a say in it.

The right side of my brain argues that I should leave and never look back. That I should realize being with someone like Lucas would bring scrutiny into my life that I don't need or want, but the right side of my brain is shadowed by the rest of my entire body, screaming that it wants to spend more time with Lucas, that auditioning for him is a sign.

Even though I promised myself when Mia got sick that I would no longer believe in signs. Some people find solace in the hope of a bigger and better plan, but the only thing I hope for is that Mia is now in a better place.

I stare at the floor and stride toward the exit without a word. The high I felt while dancing is gone and I'm left with memories of Mia at the hospital, with memories of my past mistakes.

"Jen, wait!" Lucas calls me and he jogs next to me.

"Lucas! We're not done here." His manager calls him.

"Give me one minute!" He doesn't need to yell to sound imposing.

I stop at the exit and I can't resist: I turn to him. Big mistake. Our bodies are so close to one another, I can feel his breath mixing with mine as I tilt my head up. The awe in his eyes makes me want to kiss him, to back him against the door and feel his lips against mine again. I need to reign my hormones in.

"You were absolutely amazing." His hand touches my shoulder. It's a light touch but it's enough to set my body on fire.

"Your lyrics were…they were…I'm speechless."

"Well, the girl who inspired them is pretty amazing. Full of surprises."

"I saw you…" I blurt out and wish I could take my words back when he raises an eyebrow. I lower my voice. "I don't want to get in the middle of anything. I saw you and…the girl with the red hair in the hallway and it looks like you guys are not done."

He rubs the back of his neck, but he looks more annoyed than "caught in the act." "Olivia. You saw me with Olivia," he explain as if it all made sense. "She's my ex. My manager is trying to get her back into my good graces because we make for good tabloid stories."

"Tabloid stories?"

"If tabloids report about your whereabouts, you're it. You made it. But…there's a downside to that." He chuckles and his finger trails down my cheek. I want to lean into his hand, I want to wrap my arms around him. I want…him.

"What's the downside?" I try so hard to keep my voice even but I'm clearly failing miserably because the way his eyes darken, he can feel how much I want him.

"First world problems," he jokes, but it sounds flat. He rubs the back of his neck again. Must be one of his tells when he's uncomfortable. "Sometimes, I wish they didn't print everything. Words and images hurt. One newspaper published a picture of my best friend shooting himself up a day before his death."

"What?" In his apartment, before he started baking, he told me about his best friend dying. But he never mentioned it was from an overdose.

"Lucas!" His manager sounds like my mom when she wanted me to clean my room.

"You were absolutely amazing." He bends down and his lips touch the spot right by my mouth. So close yet so far. "I'll call you."

I nod. And step out the audition room.

LOVE IN B MINOR

Because if I stayed one more minute, one more second, I would have blurted out the truth. I would have told him about that one night no one knows about except my parents.

And he would have looked at me very differently.

I almost died of an overdose too.

CHAPTER 18 - JEN

A woman with a bright smile hands me my phone and the rest of my belongings outside the audition room. "Thank you for coming!" She sounds chirpy while I feel like my heart has hit the floor and is never coming back up. My mind is racing and I almost feel dizzy. The woman must think I'm not going fast enough because she gives me a nudge. "The exit is this way. There might be callbacks, we will let you know. Have a wonderful evening."

The door slams behind my back and flashes erupt. Journalists put microphones in front of my face.

LOVE IN B MINOR

It's hard to catch my breath. Between seeing Lucas again, the heartbreaking songs, the intense dances and thinking about my past, I don't know what to say when they ask their questions in a mix of French and English.

"How was your audition? Did you see Lucas? Did he look sad? Do you know if he's back with Olivia?"

Several security guards help move the crowd of reporters and fans waiting, creating a path for me. I hadn't realized this audition was that important and I hadn't realized that Dire Blue had such a following. Signs reading *Lucas Forever* are flown in the air next to Lucas + Olivia = True Love.

They're blurry. Everything is blurry. A gust of wind slaps me across the face.

Like four years ago.

In Cape Cod.

It was the year Mia got sick. My first year at the School of Performing Arts and everything was so hard. That was before I was so good at pretending to be a bitch, to not care.

One girl tripped me on my way to class. Another managed to get a spider into my bed—I am still scared of spiders. They're my kryptonite. And they filmed me while I screamed. I got back at them the next day by drawing on their faces while they slept and filming their reactions when they woke up. That stopped them from putting it on the internet.

It was the year before Emilia got accepted, the year before I managed to create a persona. One of them made me cry by being consistently rude, by making remarks about my skin, my eyes, about my parents. When she talked about my parents, she went too far. I slapped her. She reported me to the director and I got suspended.

I worked hard. Harder every single day. The professors were demanding but I was harder on myself than anyone else. They kept pushing for more. I kept pushing for more.

By the time the holidays arrived, I was already doing coke. It's scary how easy it is to find coke when you know where to look. In my case, the dealer was a former dancer and paying for it wasn't hard since my

LOVE IN B MINOR

parents transferred a big allowance to my account each month. And I always had an excuse explaining why I was regularly falling short on funds, whenever they checked my balance. I told them I went to an expensive concert, that I needed to take extra lessons, that I was helping a friend with her tuition.

I convinced myself that doing coke was helping me. That it was enhancing my performance, making better, giving me the strength to work harder.

All lies. Everything was a lie.

In Cape Cod, I met Kane the very first morning. I went for a walk on the beach, telling myself that I was doing okay. Convincing myself that I was happy.

He was seventeen, I was almost fifteen. We kissed, we made out. He was my first kiss and the first guy I had sex with. Losing my virginity to him was not everything I thought it would be. But he was gentle and nice and made me feel like I was important.

One evening, he asked me if I wanted to chill on the beach with his friends. I said yes and then I kept on saying yes. His friends were bad news. Wealthy but bored out of their minds.

"I bet you never did heroin."

I hadn't. But I bragged about doing coke. They laughed.

The dose they gave me was too much for me. My brain fogged up. Drowsiness took over.

My breathing was too slow. Everything was too slow.

When I collapsed, they were all already gone. Even Kane.

Mom found me on the beach, called the ambulance and they sent me to rehab for the rest of the winter break. Mom and Dad looked like I had used a knife to slice their hearts. Mom couldn't stop crying over how she couldn't lose two daughters. Dad kept on looking at me like he wasn't sure who I was. Kane died a month later from a heroin overdose.

How am I supposed to tell Lucas? Even if we had a chance, if my fucked-up expectations and his own issues didn't stop us from trying, my past would make him look at me differently.

"Miss!" A security guards looks down with a concerned frown. "Are you okay?"

LOVE IN B MINOR

I wince, unable to speak. I hide my face with my bag and march through, because that's what I do. I hide my true feelings and march on.

"Jen!" Alisha calls my name from the Place de La République. She stands by the bronze statue of Marianne right by the memorial from the two terrorist attacks that happened in Paris recently. There's a teddy bear there that always catches my eye—so many deaths, so many tears, and for what?

I shake my head.

"How did it go?" I ask Alisha, who is clutching her bag tightly and whose blue eyes are wide open like she's nervous and excited and overwhelmed. "Alisha?"

"I didn't know it was the Dire Blue. And seeing Steve. He looked…"

"Still bald?" I supply, nudging her, trying to calm her down, but really using this as a way to calm myself down. If I help someone, if I focus on someone else's problems, mine might disappear for a while.

"He looked good, real good and he looked happy to see me, he looked like he was ready to jump up from his chair and embrace me." She bites her lip, which she usually only does right before stepping on stage.

"And, did he?"

"He didn't. I didn't even…I mean I said hi, I asked how he was doing and then…I danced. I was so cold. When he tried to walk me back to the door, I told him it wasn't necessary."

"Why? You looked so cozy with him on Saturday."

"That's the thing, I was cozy, way too cozy, I'm not ready," she blabbers more to herself than to me, and then she takes a deep breath. "Anyways…" She gestures to the crowd still outside the hotel. "That was something."

"It's not the first time I got photographed. But it's the first time I got photographed by dozens of paparazzi at once."

"Are you okay?" she asks, watching me carefully as if trying to catch me in a lie. "You look like Baryshnikov told you you were the worst dancer in history, which he wouldn't do because you're not."

LOVE IN B MINOR

"It was…" I purse my lips into thinking mode. Finding the right word is much harder than I thought. "Interesting."

She tilts her head to the side. "Interesting like wow, I can't believe I slept with Lucas Wills and we're totally going to date and get married and have babies, or interesting this sucks?"

"Do you have a middle ground for this interesting? Like I don't know. It was nice seeing him, he wrote a song about us, but I'm pretty sure I still don't want to get involved?"

She shrieks and tugs on my coat. "Wait, what? He wrote a song about you?"

"About our night. I think. It sounded like our night."

Her hand rises to her chest and her mouth gapes open. "This is…this is the best news ever. So exciting!"

"Not that exciting. I told you, it's not going to work."

Her eyes roam my face and her chin juts down as if I disappointed her or crushed her fantasy. "We'll see." She smiles. "By the way, didn't you notice how

Lucas Wills totally looks like that actor in that new vampire show, that revamp of *Buffy*?"

And he can quote *Parks & Rec*. And he can make me laugh like no other. And he can weaken my knees with one look. "I didn't know they were making a remake of *Buffy*." It's hard to let those words out. I want to continue talking about him. I want to ask her if she thinks he could get over my past. I want to ask her if she thinks he is over his own past.

But instead, I shrug in a noncommittal way. My favorite shrug. "His ex is still in the picture. Like she's got her claws stuck into him pretty tightly, and I'm not doing this."

"You mean, you're not doing this again. Because something definitely did happen—and it was more than an awesome night of whoopla. You wouldn't be so beside yourself if nothing had happened."

"Whoopla?" I raise an eyebrow.

"I call it whoopla. I stick by whoopla."

"Fine. Did you and Steve whoopla?"

"I told you, no. The chemistry was amazing and he seems like such a sweet guy. And I wanted to whoopla. But I didn't." She bites her lip as if preventing herself from saying more. "It's not about me, but about you. What are you going to do?" She links her arm in mine and we cross the Place de La République to the sidewalk.

"I'm going to find a place where we can sit and eat and we're not going to talk about this again."

"Sure thing," she says in an I-don't-think-so tone.

The restaurants around the Place de La République are completely full. People are laughing and talking and living.

Alisha nudges me. "We could go to St Michel."

St Michel is a neighborhood by Notre Dame. It boasts very touristy restaurants but it's an atmosphere of its own: the people calling for you to come sit inside in several languages, the smells of traditional crêperies mixed with kebabs, the crowd strolling around.

"To the Greek restaurant?" We've been to that place three times and the waiters recognize us now and even though I'm sure they do that for everyone, they always give us a little extra food and wide smiles like we're friends.

It's nice to find a spot like this when you're in a city you don't know, when you're far from your family and friends. Even in a city as gorgeous as Paris, being anonymous in the crowd only works if you have places where you're known.

"We could even take the metro, and then walk down the Boulevard so you can find more plaques to take pictures of." Her voice is stronger, and I hope I can take some of her strength to continue pretending I'm fine.

"Let's go then." Our feet take us to the metro station. It's less crowded than the time I used it during rush hour. I had to register at the consulate and thought I'd get there faster using the metro. The crowd was overwhelming and it was hard to breathe. Not this time. There are only a few dozen people in our train. The doors close and we pick up speed.

We leave Place de la République behind.

We leave this crazy evening behind.

What I would give to leave my past behind too.

CHAPTER 19 - LUCAS

As soon as the door closes on Jen, Grégoire leans back in his chair with a very loud I-can't-believe-this whistle. "Who was that girl?" he asks with an edge to his voice. "You and she clearly had a connection."

"Jen Harrison. You got her name the same time I did. I thought she was someone named Laura." I can't help being snarky. I've been holding up pretty well considering he's trying to shove my ex into the band for a music video that's supposed to put us back on the map. For a music video that is about my dead best friend.

Steve chuckles and he winks at me. Grégoire didn't give him as much crap for Alisha, but Alisha also tried really hard to not show any emotions, even though she did look like she was in pain and way too destabilized to dance in front of Steve. He didn't lose his shit when she came in. He didn't write a song about her.

Even though I hoped Jen would be there, I wasn't sure. I wasn't sure if she was a dancer, I wasn't sure if she'd come. I wasn't sure about anything.

But seeing her tonight didn't only send waves of happiness throughout my body; seeing her dance stole my breath away.

She was amazing. Simply amazing.

"She was good." Olivia's voice is almost sincere. She stands up and takes a few steps. She can't stay still when she's nervous or upset. "She was the best so far."

"You would need to work with her," Grégoire points out, and I'm not sure if he's talking to me or to her. He leans back in his chair. I hate when he gets that entitled expression on his face. Granted, he's our manager, but right now he looks like the world owes him its soul and its left nut.

"I'm a professional." She sighs and walks to the other side of the room. That used to make me laugh and I used to tease her about it. Not anymore. "Lucas has a thing for her, everyone can see it. Everyone can also guess the song is about her. The one-night stand who got away? The gossip bloggers had a field day about Lucas trying to get over us, and how he used to jump from bed to bed."

"Half of it wasn't true," I interrupt her. "And what's your point?"

"Will you be able to keep it in your pants?"

The guys snicker and I shake my head. "Again, what's your point? I didn't even agree to sing that song with you."

Olivia's shoulders drop and she glances away. I'm not used to seeing her not believing in herself, not believing everything will work her way because she's Olivia McRae.

Grégoire raises an index finger. His way of asking us to stay quiet. "The point is that you don't want to jeopardize her career and your career. Technically, you're going to be her boss if she does end up being the best today, and you know how fast that can deteriorate." He picks up her composite from her folder and very slowly reads her resume. In a way that makes me want to punch him. In a way that's so condescending that I want to call him out on it. "She's graduated from the School of Performing Arts in New York with honors and was the lead during her senior year. She started at the City of Lights Ballet Company four months ago. She has no music video experience, no show biz experience."

"We didn't say we wanted someone with music experience," I point out, unclenching my fists. Mom used to say I needed to use my words instead of fighting. And right now, words are my best bet. Maybe we can convince him.

Grégoire stares at me—with an eyebrow cocked all the way to the ceiling. I'm not the only one surprised by my calm. "You can't sleep with her."

"Can we drop my sex life as a reason why she shouldn't be hired? Plus, I can do what I want."

Grégoire shakes his head. "You know nothing about her. Plus, Olivia is right. You're technically her boss during the time she shoots the video, so it's not going to happen."

I grind my teeth and roll my eyes but still don't say a word.

Grégoire takes a pen and underlines something in the pile of papers in front of him. He does it slowly, carefully and with a smirk that tells me he knew exactly what I was thinking. "The contract states, '*Romantic or sexual relationships between members of the band and or with staff under contract where one individual has influence or control over the other's conditions of employment are inappropriate. These relationships, even if consensual, may ultimately result in conflict or difficulties in the workplace. If such a relationship currently exists or develops, it must be disclosed to the band, to the manager of the band, and to the recording label in order to decide on the best possible course of action.*'" He pauses, gives me one pointed look before continuing. "And we all know once it's disclosed to more than one person, the press is going to hear about it and once the fans become aware of it, they're going to hate her. They want you back with Olivia. Anything that goes against that will make them angry. " He shoots a glare at me, but a glare that carries all the meaning of his last sentence. Fans might hate her. And thinking about what the press did to Benji, how they destroyed him by following him around, waiting for him to slip, I don't want that for her. Grégoire smirks as if he knows he got my attention. "Now, let's all sit back down and get to the next dancer. We still have at least twenty to see. Maybe one of them will be better."

"Whatever." I sit back down next to him, glancing at Jen's picture. I read her resume and try to put meaning behind every word. It says she's been dancing since she was four years old. Did she want it? Did her parents push her? How about leaving New York?

That evening in my apartment while we were baking the cookies, I asked her why she decided to come here to learn French, why she decided to go on this adventure. I still remember her answers. *"Because where better to learn French than in France?" she first said but she didn't sound truthful. I kept on looking at her. And she bit her lower lip, tracing imaginary designs on the counter as if she was reminiscing. Then she stared right back at me. "Because sometimes, you think leaving is easier. That you can leave your worries and your sad memories behind and start fresh. It's like when you make New Year's resolutions, this idea that you can be a new you."*

"I take it you don't believe in it."

"I do. I do believe in becoming better and stronger and leaving your past in the past. But to do that, you have to be ready. I'm not quite sure I'm ready yet."

There was so much sadness in her voice. I took her hand in mine across the counter and I opened up too. *"I think there are parts of you that you don't want to change. You said earlier how much you love your family and your friends. And I saw you standing up to this guy. You were strong. Starting fresh doesn't necessarily mean forgetting who you are; maybe starting fresh is taking what you love about yourself*

and learning to smile at everything that makes you happy. Maybe it means not being afraid to be happy."

"It sounds like a song." She laughed and then leaned in, whispering, using a very self-deprecating tone: "Time is money, money is power, power is pizza, and pizza is knowledge, let's go!"

And I laughed at her ability to quote *Parks & Rec*, before kissing her and finally ordering the pizza.

I don't even bother to hide my smile.

"Are you done looking at her picture and daydreaming?" Grégoire shoots me a death glare that he believes has me shitting in my pants. He couldn't be more wrong.

Linda—the director's assistant—who wears piercings like a statement chimes in. "Should I call the next dancer? We still have twenty-five girls to see."

"I thought it was twenty," Steve mutters while Dimitri yawns loudly.

"I'm ready." I cross my arms on my chest. Telling myself I will give them all a fair chance and that if one of them is better than Jen, she'll get the role.

But they're not.

LOVE IN B MINOR

The rest of the auditions are pretty much the same over and over again. Even though I'm impressed by all the talent that showed up, I'm not impressed with *them*. I don't get lost in the way they move. I don't believe them, the way I believed Jen.

Then, there are some who are clearly not dancers and just wanted to see who was auditioning. I'm guessing that's Grégoire's doing. Putting a hint or two in some non-specialized press so some groupies show up. One was disappointed it was us, though—she was expecting One Direction.

Oh well.

Another stripped instead of dancing.

And then jumped on the table, screaming how much she wanted to become famous.

I'm worried about that one. I asked one of the security guards to double check on her and make sure she got home okay.

After the last one exits the room, Grégoire stands up. If he thinks that by towering over me, he will be more convincing, he's wrong.

"Before deciding, I'd like to make sure we're all on the same page, and I want to hear Olivia and Lucas sing the song from the video."

"I haven't made up my mind yet." I don't need to raise my voice to sound pissed. "This song doesn't need a second singer."

"You mean it doesn't need *me* as a second singer," Olivia chimes in. Her light brown eyes flash with anger and pain. "You know I could make this song great. You know how much Benji meant to me too."

"You didn't even know the song was about him." I'm tempted to say she thought it was about her, but humiliating her in front of the others isn't my style.

Dimitri raises his hand. "I understand you guys have issues, but two things. One, can we hear Olivia sing that song with you before making any decisions? Two, Jen was clearly the best. She blew us all away and she would be great on video."

Grégoire smiles his I-know-I-won smile. "Not only do I think it's a great idea to listen to the both of you sing that song, I also believe that Benji's grandmother would like to see you two sing something for your best friend. Together. Like old times."

I have to hold on to my chair to not jump on him and beat him up. Bringing up Benji's grandmother now? It's lower than I thought he would ever get. Who is to say she would even recognize us? She's got more bad days than good ones.

But Olivia surprises me for the second time in less than half an hour. "I want to sing. But I understand if you don't want me to. I get it. I screwed up. I fucking screwed up."

"Oh yeah you did," Steve whispers. He wasn't even a band member when it all went down, but he was one of the few who helped pick up the pieces.

"But even though Grégoire was being an ass, he was right about Benji's grandmother. We could sing together one last time. For him and for her."

Part of me wants to say yes. Before we became somewhat famous, it was always the three of us. Olivia, Benji and I. Olivia and I met at the American School of Paris. Benji didn't go there. His grandmother didn't have enough money to afford the tuition, and they lived on the outskirts of Paris, but Benji liked to play soccer close by our school at night. He used to bet with the rich kids he could beat them and he usually did. We were fourteen and became inseparable. Especially when we found out we both loved music. Olivia always wanted to sing and even though she admitted her voice wasn't the best, she brought passion and commitment. Olivia and I booked the music room every night at school and we would sneak Benji in. It was the three of us living our dream.

"We could remember him that way and make people remember something other than his last month." His spiraling-down hell. She's not saying it but it's in her eyes.

I thought it was the best time of our lives, but now when I look back, I see the little things I brushed aside before. How Benji struggled with the fact his only family—his grandmother—was forgetting about him, calling him by his dad's name. A dad he'd never even met. How Benji tried so hard to fit in. How he sometimes looked at Olivia like she hung the moon.

LOVE IN B MINOR

He never told me he had fallen for her, but if I'm being entirely honest with myself, I knew he had. He never told me how much he was hurting. But I should have known. The alcohol, the drugs. They didn't come with the beginning of the fame, they were there before, they were just much easier to get once we hung out in certain clubs, got our pictures taken, became somewhat famous. Benji was drowning and I didn't even see it.

"Okay." My voice is strong and sure even though I feel miserable.

"What?" everyone says at once, more surprised than I thought.

"Let's try it. Let's see how it works. With the vocals. But it's just that one song. For him. For Benji."

"Tomorrow at the studio?" Olivia asks and she sounds so hopeful, even desperate. I look at her more carefully but she's got a blank mask on.

"Okay." I cross my arms behind my head. "Now, do we all agree that Jen should get the part?" I turn to the side to challenge Grégoire to disagree, but he doesn't.

165

"Let me announce it tomorrow," he replies instead. "I'd like to give an exclusive to Fran Gaves. She runs the top gossip blog in the US and she started developing one in France."

"I'd like to tell Jen first," I reply. And not because I want to talk to her soon again.

"What if she blabbers to the press?"

"She won't." I can pretend to be sure of something I'm definitely not. Because who am I to say she's going to keep it to herself? I spent one night with her and even though I hate feeling that way, I do need to make sure she's not like Olivia. That she won't use me.

Grégoire sighs, dismissively. "Fine. I need you all to come to a party tonight and she can't join until it's been announced. I'll meet Fran at the Cloche Du Roi restaurant at twelve thirty and I'll get her to release the news by two thirty so we hit the evening buzz on social media in the US."

"I'll tell her tomorrow morning then." I grab her paperwork and check for her cell phone number. Or maybe I should pass by and tell her. I enter her address just in case. "You need to make sure she actually accepts before announcing it anyways. I'll bring her the contract." I'm pretty impressed with the way I still appear professional even though what I'm really wondering is: *Will she agree to see me? How about going out with me? How about how her face fell right before we said goodbye earlier today like something was bothering her?*

"It's settled then." Grégoire stands up. "The party is in Club D on the Champs-Élysées. You all need to show up, including you, Olivia. We need to get the crowd wondering about a possible reunion. When you left for your solo career splitting up the band, a lot thought you might come back for some songs, but with all the drama…" He glances in my direction, pursing his lips, waiting for me to explode like I usually do when he brings up Olivia, but I'm not going to. If we sing that song in Benji's memory, we need to at least not be at each other's throats.

For Benji.

"I'll be there."

And when I leave the hotel by myself—I refused Grégoire's suggestion that Olivia and I come out together—I smile at the photographers, sign a few autographs, discreetly looking behind the crowd, on the sidewalk, in the restaurants. Chances are slim she stuck around for such a long time, but I still look. Because seeing her again had to be a sign. I'm not sure what type of sign, but a sign that our story can't end with a one-night stand.

Benji would not only agree, he would approve. He always believed in signs. And tarot cards, and looking into the stars.

None of the psychics he saw told him he was going to die at eighteen from too much heroin.

CHAPTER 20 – JEN

The excitement of the day is slowly waning off. Alisha and I found a plaque on the Boulevard Saint Michel that I hadn't photographed yet. One about Jean Montvallier-Boulogne, a twenty-four-year-old who died in 1944 during the Liberation. Paris has endured so much throughout the centuries; maybe that's why it seems so resilient. Maybe that's why it's so fascinating.

We ate in the small Greek restaurant in the 11th arrondissement, and we talked about the company, about her dreams, about important things but not dangerous ones. Dangerous topics like my past, and my demons.

I didn't confide to her about my past. I didn't tell her how much seeing Lucas again scares me, because reality is usually so much more screwed up than all the fantasies in my head.

As soon as I'm back in my apartment, I get comfy: large sweatpants, a sweater from the School of Performing Arts, big fuzzy socks. I take out my cell phone and put it to charge. Right away it beeps with a voice mail.

I sit down at my computer.

It's almost ten p.m.

Four in the afternoon in the city. I turn on Skype, but my parents are rarely on. Em isn't either. She's either taking a power nap after waking up at three in the morning to prepare sweets for their new bakery, or she's gone to see Nick.

I could google Lucas now. I could check all the stories, check what his past with that girl is, and what happened to his friend, but I don't. Because I want him to tell me—I don't want to take away his decision to tell me. And I have a feeling, even though he seems grateful for the spotlight and success, there are a few aspects that destroyed him.

I click on Mom's profile and call her cell phone. "Hi, honey." She actually picks up, which has me all sorts of confused. She's usually busy at this time.

"Hey. Where are you?"

"Running errands. I finished work early and I'm going to surprise your dad with dinner."

"You sound good."

"You don't." There's shuffling in the background, honking. "You sound sad, is everything okay?"

"I don't know." The words tumble out. I didn't mean to be blunt. But hearing concern in my mother's voice is disconcerting and I wasn't prepared for that.

"Your dad and I have been talking a lot these recent days. And we know it hasn't been easy for you either. And we know we haven't been there."

I'm going to cry at my computer. I'm going to lose it right here and now. There's so much sadness in me I don't know what to do with it. "I…" My voice cracks. "I know it was hard for you too."

"Yes. It was and it still is. And part of us will always miss your little sister. Part of us will always wonder if we could have done anything differently, tried another course of chemo. Anything. But… Wait, honey, let me get in the car." A door opens and closes. Probably our usual driver picking her up. "What I'm trying to say is that we didn't forget about you. It's just we were both grieving in different ways, and part of us didn't want to bring you down with us."

"But I wasn't there." This time I can't stop the tears from falling down.

"You were. You were there. You called every single day. We didn't know that it was going to happen when it did. Baby, you tried everything. You postponed your entry into the ballet company until they gave you an ultimatum and Mia told you to go." Mom sounds like she actually believes what she's saying, that she actually believes I'm not guilty of abandoning them.

"I wanted to be there. If I had known…"

LOVE IN B MINOR

"Again, you were there. In every phone call, in every video you sent, in every little thing you did even when you weren't close by, you were there." She clears her throat. "You came back as soon as you could. And Mia knew you loved her."

"I miss her. I miss her so much." And I continue to cry, tears I haven't let myself feel in a very long time.

"I know. And I want you to be able to talk to me about it. To me or to your dad. Or to a therapist." She pauses and I'm not sure if it's so she doesn't cry too, or if she's thinking about the way to phrase her next sentence. "Are you doing okay otherwise? With everything?"

And I know what she's asking between the lines. She wants to know if I used anything again, if I went down the dark path because I couldn't cope.

"I'm doing okay. I was thinking about calling Dr. Archer to see if he could refer me to someone in Paris."

"That could be a good idea. And honey?"

"Hmm."

"Your dad and I will be there for your next show. And we will call you next week, okay?"

"Okay, Mom. I love you."

"We love you too." And she hangs up. And my heart's fuller than it's been in such a long time. I don't know what brought them to talking about the situation more, or how they started working on it, but hearing Mom like this gives me hope that maybe everything will be okay. For months, I was scared they would split up because I've read this happens a lot in those situations. People not able to connect and to grieve a child together, and I wondered how they would do without each other. My parents fought so much for their own relationship, they fought so much for my sister, and for me.

Maybe, I can tell Lucas about what happened to me and he won't freak out, he won't leave me behind.

Maybe I can take a chance.

But before, I need to write to Dr. Archer and get that referral.

CHAPTER 21 - LUCAS

The club is full. It's one of those clubs that's full of fancy lighting and modern furniture. The type of club that tries hard to pretend it's not cool but overdoes it. The type of club I hate.

The music is so loud I have to lean in to listen to Steve and I only make out a few words he's slurring. He's hammered. Or maybe I'm hammered.

I lean in even closer, my ear almost touching his mouth, and laughter bubbles within me. Because that's funny. He's blabbering about that Alisha girl, and how she won't return his calls.

"You have to ask Jen about her. See if she has someone maybe or…"

"I thought you didn't grovel after girls. That they came to you, not the other way around."

"Come on, please…." He sounds whiny, and it's very unlike Steve to sound whiny.

I laugh and down another shot. I haven't texted Jen to tell her but I did try to call her. She didn't pick up. Maybe it was too late. Maybe it is too late. Maybe I drank too much. And I drink another shot.

The beginning of the evening was pretty tame. I told myself I'd only make an appearance, have a few drinks and then go home early. But I made the mistake of listening to some girl talking about how she met Benji before he died, and what a great guy he was, and how sad it was he died. It wouldn't have been as hard if she didn't finish with: "We saw it coming though. He was really going down a dark path."

I didn't see it coming. I had staged an intervention two months prior to his death and I thought it had worked okay. I thought it was going to be easy for him to stop using drugs. One stern talk from all of us. Support and a quick stint in rehab and all his problems would be gone. But it wasn't easy and I didn't see it.

The music changes and I force myself to pretend to be happy, to pretend to not drown in my thoughts and memories.

I stand up and get to the middle of the room where people grind against each other. I sway my hips from side to side, then raise my fist up in the air and jump. I don't care what people think. I'm here to pretend to have a good time.

"Oh hey goodbye!" I sing at the top of my lungs. Olivia dances close by and then, she trips and I catch her. Cameras flash and I give them the finger. Because intoxicated me is clearly the bigger person. "I got to go," I tell her.

And she smiles. "Do you want me to come with you?"

I shake my head. "Nope. Nope. Not you. Definitely not you, but thank you." Her face falls but she keeps her smile on—probably for all the photographers. "But you can help me distract them." I nod toward the vultures.

"How?"

"I'm sure you can find something. You were always good at make-believe." The words sound a bit harsh but I kiss her cheek to soften the blow. "Thank you. I owe you one." Olivia and I have known each for so long. So long. Again, the cameras flash.

Olivia's smile turns into a grimace which may look natural to everyone but me. It's her *I'm not happy* forced smile. But she still leans in, giving me a very good view of her boobs. They almost spill out of her top, but they don't do anything to me. She doesn't do anything to me.

I need to get out.

She whispers in my ear. "Fine, but you do owe me one. Now, let me put on a show." And she jumps up, clapping her hands like she's the happiest person on Earth, and she calls up to Grégoire. "Grégoire! Grégoire, come on, you have no idea what Lucas just told me!" She's loud. Super loud. Everyone turns their attention to her. And I use the moment to wobble toward the bathroom, which also has another exit. I grab my phone and dial my driver's number. "Hey Mathieu, *tu peux venir me chercher*?" When I have too much to drink, I fluctuate between French and English, it can be hard to follow me apparently. "I'm getting out of Club D—that new disco on the Champs-Élysées. I'll be in the back."

And I slip out. Man it's cold. And dark. And what time is it? It's not even midnight yet. Maybe I could pass by Jen's and tell her the good news. Or maybe not. Maybe it's too late. Or maybe if she's awake. Maybe I should call her again. Or text her.

Yeah, I'll text her. *Hi Laura/Jen...*

After one second, she answers. *Hi Clement/Lucas. So, you're the number who called me several times. Sorry, I was with my mom on the phone. I wanted to tell you. I loved your song. I loved every word of your song.*

My car pulls next to the curb and I slide into it, almost bumping my head on the ceiling. Because clearly texting and walking is a hazard. *Are you awake?*

No. I'm typing in my sleep. Of course I'm awake.

And I laugh. Because she's right. And maybe because the last shot may have been a bit too much. *I'm on my way.*

What?

Be there in five minutes. Good news.

Good news that you'll be there in five minutes?

No, no. I have good news.

And I lean back against the leather seat. "Can you take me to this address?" I show Jen's address to my driver.

"Should I wait for you once we're there?"

"I'll take a cab home. Don't worry." My mouth tastes weird and forming sounds is much harder than before.

"Mister Sarant has asked me to make sure you get home safely."

"Grégoire is not my father. I'll be fine." And I close my eyes—until the car stops again.

"We're here."

LOVE IN B MINOR

For a second, my brain scrambles to find reasons not to get out of the car. Rushing to Jen because I'm feeling down isn't something I should get used to, right? Rushing to Jen because I'm dying to see her again is risky—I don't know her. I'm not sure what she wants, where she's at.

"Do you want me to keep driving?" Matthieu asks me slowly, like I may not understand.

"No. I'm getting out." I struggle to open the door and to read the numbers of the buildings. She lives in 12 rue Voltaire. There. But I forgot to write which apartment.

I take out my phone. She sent me several messages but there's no time to read them. *Which one is your apartment?*

When she doesn't answer, I sway to the side and sing. Maybe a bit too loudly. A window opens and an older lady screams in French. "You got to leave or I'm calling the police. I need to sleep!"

Oops. Someone else could have recognized me.

Another window opens. This time the voice warms my heart and my entire body. "Oh my god, stop singing. I'm buzzing you in."

CHAPTER 22 - JEN

I can't believe he was outside singing. He sounds drunk. His texts sounded drunk. And what the heck am I going to do with a drunk Lucas?

Someone could have seen him enter, and then could have called the press. I so do not need anyone to scrutinize my life. I slam the window shut and bite the inside of my cheek. My apartment isn't a mess, but it's sad and pathetic. I don't even have enough dishes to invite friends over. Even though Mom thinks I bought them. The next time she comes to visit she's going to be disappointed.

I wipe my eyes before buzzing him in. No time to at least try to look decent. Oh well. "Third floor." I'm proud my voice isn't as needy and lost as I feel.

He knocks loudly and I don't think before opening to him. Because if I paused and stepped back to analyze the situation, I would know that this could be a terrible mistake.

"Can I come in?" His voice sends a warm tingle down my spine. His deep voice. The one I don't think I'll ever forget after listening to him sing and talk and sing again. His hair is tousled, like someone ran their fingers through it several times. And right when I'm thinking this, he runs his fingers through his hair, and I smile one of those smiles that only he instigates. It's a happy I-can't-help-it smile.

"You look beautiful."

I open the door wider, to let him in. "And you stink."

"I drank. A little. A lot." Our arms brush as he enters. Our arms brush and my heart skips a beat. Maybe talking in the hallway would not be such a bad idea. But someone could recognize him and there's a sadness surrounding him that I can't bear. "You had no clue who I was." It sounds like a question, like he wants to make sure of a detail I'm not entirely sure I understand.

"I pretty much only watch Netflix." I walk to my tiny kitchen; my steps seem all wrong, like my feet know he's watching me and they're trying to impress him but they can't. My movements are all wrong. I'm too aware of him.

Stopping in front of the cabinets, I pull out a glass, anything to prevent me from looking at him right now. If I did, he'd probably see how much I want him, how much it scares me, how much I have no clue what I'm doing. "Do you want some water? I think you need water. Or coffee. Something other than tequila."

I swear I can hear him smile. Or maybe it's the way he answers with a little twang in his voice that wasn't there before. "You're probably right. I think you're right."

I'm not sure I'm going to be able to make small talk. He plops himself on my couch. "Your apartment is empty."

"I have a couch. A bed. A table and chairs." I sound defensive even though he's right. I know he's right. My apartment doesn't necessarily look like a lived-in place.

"I like the drawing on that wall. It's pretty."

I don't need to look to know what drawing he's talking about—it's the one Mia made for me the day she told me I needed to go to Paris. There's a plane and an Eiffel Tower and we're both smiling. "My sister made that drawing for me."

"You said your sister was gone…in my apartment, you said…she passed away but…you said…no talking about it." He sounds tired and his words blur together. He takes off his jacket, frowns and his face is so sad that I want to go and hug him. But even though we slept together, I'm not sure I should. So, instead, I pat his hand very awkwardly. "Here, drink some water." I give him the glass and he gulps it down.

"More?" he asks and I laugh because what else am I supposed to do?

I get up and pour him another glass.

LOVE IN B MINOR

"So…you mentioned the other night your mom is French and your dad is American?"

I have no clue if he'll be able to talk but I think he needs to distract himself from whatever thoughts are bringing him down.

"Yep. It was love at first sight. Dad came to France to study at La Sorbonne, he met my mother one morning while he was exploring Versailles. She was his guide—she was studying to become a history professor and working there on weekends. He wanted to be the curator of Le Louvre at some point. They got married six months later."

"Wow."

"One of those stories you see in movies. We lived in the US until I was thirteen and then when Mom got a job opportunity in France, Dad decided we should take the plunge." He takes the glass of our water and this time, when our fingers touch, my heart doesn't only skip a beat, a delicious tingle spreads though my entire body. He still sounds hammered but maybe more tired than drunk now. "I didn't like it at first. But the

American School was fun and they had lots of music. That's where…Olivia."

"Olivia," I repeat.

"She's my ex." Too bad his eyes are closed because he's missing some major eye rolling action.

I remember who Olivia is. Of course I do. She's one of the reasons why this…us…this thing right now is a very bad idea.

"We're not together. Anymore. She…she used me." I hate the disappointment in his voice. And again, I'm reminded that maybe he still cares for her, more than he realizes.

I sit back away from him a little and he opens his eyes.

There's hurt and there's passion.

But most of all there's a whole lot of pain.

CHAPTER 23– LUCAS

I'm not in my bed. I'm not in my bed and my head is pounding. The strong smell of fresh-brewed coffee is overpowering. And my stomach lurches. Man, I drank too much last night. The last thing I remember is trying to kiss Jen and her gently pushing me away. I can't believe I tried to make out with her while I was so wasted I probably didn't even remember my birthday.

The front door opens and Jen enters, carrying a bag from a bakery. "I brought croissants. They're buttery and fat, so it could help with your hangover."

"Did I tell you last night that I thought seeing you again was a sign?"

"Maybe."

"And did I really make a move on you?"

"A move which was very hard to resist. You can be very convincing." She smiles and her entire face lights up. "Don't worry. You weren't too bad."

"Not too bad."

"And you did tell me I got the part in the music video, so that's a plus."

"We didn't…" I gesture to the bed, feeling like the biggest jerk on the entire planet.

"Nope. I slept on the couch, while you took my bed. You didn't claim it as much as falling into it, really." She steps forward and hands me a croissant. "I've got to go to rehearsal in about thirty minutes. You said something last night about Grégoire needing to talk to some blog gossip lady first to make the big announcement."

"That's right." I stand up and she purses her lips before giggling.

"You might want to put clothes on."

LOVE IN B MINOR

"What?" I look down and I'm baring everything. And I can't hide the fact that I'm happy to see her. "How?" I grab the sheet and cover myself, but now her giggle has turned into a full-out laugh, including one tiny snort she doesn't even bother to hide, and I love the sound of it.

"Last night, you decided you were hot and then you said something about no longer hiding and being your true self and you took off your clothes."

"I have a feeling I should get the jerk of the night award."

"Nah, you were cute and you were sad at the beginning. We talked for a long time and it was nice."

"Nice enough for you to reconsider giving me a chance? I do remember you telling me you didn't want to get in the middle of Olivia and me."

"We'll see. How about first we, I don't know…hang out? And do that video together, and then we'll see."

"So, you want to do that video together first." I don't like the sound of that. I remember Grégoire's words, how we don't really know Jen, how maybe she

ELODIE NOWODAZKIJ

knew who I was. But even if she did, she's the best dancer for the part, and I can't believe I'm doubting her after she took such good care of me last night.

"Your phone is beeping. Quite insistently." Jen picks up my phone, which for some reason ended up on the floor last night.

"It's Grégoire," I tell her. "And I've got a message from Olivia."

Grégoire calls again. And he can be persistent. "Where are you?" He sounds upset, but again when does Grégoire not sound upset?

"I'm at Jen's. Why?"

"You haven't seen your emails yet?"

"Nope. It's seven in the morning. My head is killing me."

"Well, your head might be killing you more once you found out what *Stardom Magazine* has printed this morning."

"What?"

"It's a picture of you and Olivia kissing."

"Kissing? Olivia? What?" I turn to Jen and she furrows her brows, staring down at the floor and stepping away from me. "I didn't kiss Olivia last night." I repeat, this time for Jen's sake, "I did not."

"You can do whatever you want," she mutters. "That's why we're friends. Friends is good."

"Did Olivia spread the rumors?"

"No, she did not. She called the newspaper up herself and said this was a lie; she's also quoted in another online magazine saying that you were kissing her on the cheek to say goodbye and that you guys are not back together."

"I'm impressed."

"I don't think she's playing games anymore. She's learned her lesson. And I don't think publicity— any publicity—is bad, as you know, but what I don't want is another love triangle."

"Another?"

"You know what I mean." And I do, and it hurts. Because the gossip magazines had picked up on the time Olivia and Benji spent together, they twisted everything and when Benji died from an overdose, they called it the end of a tragic love triangle.

Bullshit. So much bullshit.

"Fine, whatever. There's nothing. Because Olivia and I are nothing anymore. Friendly exes, that's our aim."

"What you say goes," Grégoire replies. "Don't forget I'm telling Fran at twelve thirty, so make sure your Jen doesn't blabber until the news gets out at two thirty on her blog."

"She won't say anything." I hang up, feeling even more hungover than before, or maybe just more frustrated, angry.

I find my boxers on the side of the bed and put my jeans back on, trying to make eye contact with Jen, but she's keeping busy, cleaning a counter that already looks spotless.

"Apparently, the media is having a field day with me kissing Olivia on the cheek."

"You don't have to explain." She shakes her head, and her long black hair flies around. She gathers it to her head and ties it into a knot. I've noticed she's done that before, usually when she's trying to keep busy, or trying to push me away, to keep me at distance. "Really, you don't."

LOVE IN B MINOR

"But I feel like I do."

"Last night, when you were drunk, you told me you agreed with me. That being friends would be good. That you needed a friend."

"Did I say that after my failed pathetic attempt at kissing you?"

"You kissed my shoulder. You were getting tired at that point." When she smiles, I don't see it in her eyes; it's like half of her is there, and the other half is gone somewhere I can't reach her.

"Why don't you want to give us a try?" I rub the back of my neck and when she turns to me, her mouth forms a small "o" as she keeps her eyes trained on my body before reaching my face. I know I'm not letting her indifferent. Hell, the night we spent together was not only fun, it was also hot, full of passion. You can't fake that kind of passion.

She shuffles around and then gets my shirt from underneath a pillow on the couch. "Here, maybe you want to put that on."

"Why?"

"Because I can't think straight when you're half naked in my apartment."

"You're attracted to me."

She rolls her eyes like I've stated the obvious. "Of course. I usually don't sleep with strangers I'm not attracted to."

"You like me."

And this time, she tilts her head, steps forward, like she wants to be closer to me. I'm not objecting. Not one bit. "I do like you."

"So, what's the issue?"

"I've got something to tell you." She shifts her weight from one foot to the other. "Well, first, I don't want to get in the middle."

"But you're not."

"That's what you say but there are signs I recognize. The fact that you still care about Olivia."

"I think I always will. She was a part of my life for so long and even though she screwed up, I know she wasn't the only one. I screwed up too."

"You're not hearing what I'm saying."

"You're afraid I still love her."

LOVE IN B MINOR

She tilts her head back. "Okay, maybe you're hearing what I'm saying."

"What other reasons do you have?"

"We're going to be working together for several weeks at least. Grégoire sent me an email about doing some promo together, some live shows where you'll be singing and I'll be dancing. You also showed me the contract last night and it could get really awkward, especially if we don't work out."

"Not more awkward than singing for my dead friend with the girl who lied to me and who everyone believed had something going with him." I raise one eyebrow because I know I got her there.

She gasps. "What?"

"Long story short, Benji and Olivia were spending a lot of time together. Without me. And rumors spread about them maybe sleeping together behind my back. Benji denied it. Olivia cried. Whatever."

"I'm so sorry," she whispers and her hand runs down my arm soothingly. I stare at it. Usually, I joke when I'm being shown one ounce of compassion or pity, because I don't think I deserve it, because I don't think I was there enough for Benji. But her touch is intoxicating, like she understands me. Like she knows what I'm going through and wants to help.

"There's something else." She hesitates and there's so much fear in her eyes that I breach the distance between us and pull her to me.

"I get it, you're scared, and I don't want to force you to do anything you don't want to. If you want to be friends first, that's fine by me. If you can look past the gossip and the pressure and my past."

"Your past?"

"After Olivia, I kind of went overboard with enjoying the attention I was getting."

"Is that code for you slept around?"

"A lot." I kiss the top of her head and am so tempted to run my hands underneath her silky cream-colored shirt. Her skin is smooth, darker than mine, and I love the way she feels. "Listen, I'm going to get out of your way, let you go talk to the director of your ballet company. Remind him, he can't say anything until mid-afternoon, or Grégoire is going to lose it. Big time."

LOVE IN B MINOR

She opens her mouth but I continue. "We'll talk about this again. Maybe tonight?"

"Tonight?"

"If your director is okay, we're going to go over the script later this afternoon." I slap my forehead and then wince, because the pain is still pretty strong. "I forgot, I'm supposed to ask you about your friend...Alisha."

"Steve asked you?" She smiles and this time it's genuine and it takes all my self-control to not steal a kiss, because she's still so close, so warm, so soft and sweet.

"He did. It seemed Alisha really impressed him, but she kind of pushed him away."

"I can get the story from her. At least, try to. She seemed to like him, but she kind of closed up fast when we talked about it."

I wrap my arms tighter around her and lift her off the floor for a bear hug, kiss the top of her head again, then her cheek and her neck... she doesn't stiffen in my arms, instead there's a throaty sound that gets me instantly hard. I let her back down and mumble, "I'll see you later…" before gathering my clothes, wallet and phone in a hurry.

Once I'm out, I take a deep breath.

She surprises me by opening the door again, with the bag of croissants. "Here, take one at least, you're going to need it."

And she's right.

CHAPTER 24 – JEN

I could have melted in Lucas' arms. Melted right there. Melted and not even regretted it. He's got this tough look about him: in the way his jaw hardens when he's upset, in the way his muscles flex, in the way he closes up. Or maybe it's the tattoo. When he was without his shirt, all I wanted was to reach out and trace the shape of the birds flying away, but I can't do that. Not until I tell him the truth.

I wanted to. I really wanted to. I was about to, but he cut me off and the way he looked at me, like I was special and couldn't do any wrong…

ELODIE NOWODAZKIJ

My heart screams it's not real, my brain screams
we need to show each other our weaknesses if we really
want to give each other a chance, but can I enjoy this
phase a bit longer? He already knows me better than a
lot of my so-called friends. The only other people who
have seen beyond the surface are Em and now Alisha. I
thought Nick did too, but he was too busy dealing with
his own demons and with Emilia's to really dig deeper
into my issues. And I didn't want to let him.

I finally move away from the kitchen and plop
down at my computer. My therapist gave me the name
of a colleague who works in Paris and is American.
Doing therapy in French wouldn't have worked as well.
I enter the number in my phone and Google him. His
office says it opens at 7:30 a.m. So I leave a message.

I grab my coffee and sip on it, taking a bite of
the croissant I picked up at the bakery around the
corner—they were still warm when I got them. I've
only had croissants three times since I've arrived and
they're still as delicious, melting in your mouth. With
one hand, I log into my emails.

An email from Em.

LOVE IN B MINOR

Hi Jen,

How are you? I know I texted you yesterday but I had to update you on the salt/sugar situation at the culinary school. The guy who did that also tried to mess with my flour. Luckily I saw him before we started baking, otherwise I would have been screwed. Except for that little healthy competition (as the director calls it), I've been doing well. I miss you though. Yes, I know, you don't want all the mushy stuff but see, I think you do, you're just too afraid to admit it, which brings me to my next point: have you met someone?

Oh, I also wanted to share that meme I found online the other day, I know it's going to make you laugh.

I got to go. Call me maybe?

☺

Emilia.

The meme she sent me is of a ballerina screaming at her director. And it does make me smile because I'd give anything to put Igor back in his place. I make a mental note to reply to her later today. I still can't believe Em and I moved past all of our issues to actually become friends. Granted, Nick came between us, but the main reason I was always so angry with her was because I knew she didn't want to be dancing, and she was taking the spot of someone who might really want to make a career out of it and couldn't.

There's a short email from my dad telling me he loves me and that they'll call next Sunday. I can't wait to tell them about the video and even though I'm still wondering what brought their change of heart and their desire to work on themselves, I'm all for it. I could learn one or two things from them.

My computer dings with another email. It's from Grégoire. I scratch my temple—what does he want? He doesn't seem to be a fan of mine, at least I didn't get that impression during the auditions.

Subject: Important – Contract/Communication

Jennifer,

I'd like to ensure that you understand the terms of the contract when it comes to communication. You are not allowed to give any types of interviews or

LOVE IN B MINOR

background talks about your work with Dire Blue. If
you do, this will be found in breach of contract and you
will not receive payment. In addition, we would be
obliged to bring you in front of the court for possible
defamation.

Please read the article attached to understand
what I mean when it comes to dealing with the media.
We would not want Lucas or the band to find
themselves in the midst of a scandal which could hurt
their chances.

I look forward to working with you.
Grégoire.

I click on the pdf he attached. It's a screenshot
of the article which was published last night, the one
that had Lucas all up in arms.

There's a picture of Lucas leaning toward Olivia
as if he's kissing her. I know he hasn't. I believe him. I
believe what he said but my stomach still plummets to
the floor like a ballerina who can't land a *grand jeté*.
Because it hits home and because what if some
journalist ends up finding out about my overdose?

There was no article in the press and I don't have a record, because my parents made sure of it, but what if someone still remembers me, and they dig through everything?

Lucas would know. Everyone would know.

Promise me you're going to fall in love. Mia's words come back to haunt me. *Promise me you're going to love. Like Beauty. Like all the princesses. You've got to pinky swear.*

Words are easy but actions are so much harder. What happened was more than four years ago, and even though my therapist managed to convince me I don't have to keep on punishing myself for it, I'm not sure that past isn't coming back and ruining everything.

CHAPTER 25 – LUCAS

The ride back to my place is quiet. I close my eyes in the car and take a little nap. Even though my life is all about going out, showing my face, performing, it's still been a while since I drank that much.

The driver clears his throat, probably to wake me up gently. "Should I take you to your place or do you want to go anywhere else?"

"To my apartment, please." And thoughts race through my mind. Sleeping is not going to be possible. We drive past the club where I first laid eyes on Jen and pride bursts within me as I remember how she stood up to that guy, as if she was ready to fight, even though it was clear afterwards that it was the adrenaline working.

I scratch my nose. Thinking that Grégoire walked by without even asking if she needed any help baffles me. Benji told me once it used to be his routine. Asking for help but no one caring. Acting out so someone would care. He thought if he made enough noise his parents would come back for him. But they never did. His grandma told him his mom died giving birth to him, and his father couldn't deal with the pain so he ran off. He never even called for Benji's birthday or anything. Benji loved his grandmother fiercely, but he still wanted more. He said he got the "more" he'd been looking for when Olivia and I ran into him at that soccer field by the American School of Paris.

But it wasn't enough. If we had been enough, he would not have died.

The pain over his death comes and goes in waves. The guilt eats me. "Can you turn on the radio, please?" I need noise to drown my thoughts.

"Sure, what station?"

LOVE IN B MINOR

"Europe 1." At this hour, that station has the news, guests coming. It will distract me until we're home. Some days, I feel like the guilt will win. Other days, it's the anger. The anger of not realizing how far he'd gone. Then I'm also angry at him. Too many emotions and not one clear winner.

Outside, people are going on with their lives. Cars honk every few minutes, people hurry on the sidewalk to their destination. The buildings stand— they've seen wars and they've seen lovers. They've seen everything and they still stand. Some date from the Middle Ages. They keep on standing through fire and floods.

And that's what I should do. I need to keep on standing and living. Because living is also a way to honor Benji's memory, living my dreams.

That evening with Jen, I felt alive for the first time in months. I don't think it's because she didn't know who I was, but because she paid attention. She listened and she cared. She made me laugh. She let me talk without expecting anything.

I can't complain about being successful. Hell, I've always wanted to be a singer, a performer, ever since Dad took me backstage at a Blood concert when I was little. He had gone to high school with one of the guys working with them, and they reconnected on Facebook. When Dad told him I played the piano and loved to sing, the guy told Dad he should nurture my talents.

Dad and Mom enrolled me in music lessons, voices lessons, but my real beginning was with Olivia and Benji. Olivia and I wrote music together, we sang, we played at school events, at our parents' parties. Benji brought a different touch. He had learned the guitar on one of his old grandfather's guitars by watching YouTube videos and taught himself to play the piano at the local community center. He could harmonize like no other. He could replay a song he heard only twice. He had an ear and an aura.

He simply got lost.

Lost in the newfound fame, lost in his dreams and lost in finding himself alone after his grandma got diagnosed with Alzheimer. His troubles began when he was little. He was pushing for attention, the only way he knew how.

"Lucas?" The driver says my name like he maybe had to repeat it a few times. "We're blocking part of the road." His other way of telling me that I probably should get my ass out of the car.

"Of course."

"Do I need to pick you up at one thirty to be at the studio?"

"That would be great." I could take the metro and lose myself in the crowd. With sunglasses and a hat, people simply walk by me without recognizing me. But Grégoire usually freaks out. He's told me before he wanted to hire a full-time bodyguard, a full-time security service for us. But for now, I don't think it's necessary. "Thanks again," I tell the driver before entering the building.

Once in the apartment, I sit down at the piano, play a few songs. My mind races through the hangover fog. Singing with Olivia isn't such a bad idea. My eyes find the frame on the bookshelf. I never had the heart to take it out. Olivia and Benji smile one of their happy smiles.

My phone rings and I hesitate before picking up because I'm sure Mom saw the headlines and is worried Olivia and I are back together, worried I'm going to get hurt again. However, if I don't pick up, she's going to be even more worried and probably will come here herself to make sure I'm okay.

"Bonjour Maman," I say in French.

"You're on loudspeaker. Your dad is with me." She sounds out of breath. My dad speaks almost perfect French, but for some reason they talk in English to one another. Maybe because they lived in the US for such a long time after meeting. "What's going on? That picture in that magazine." She sneers at the word "magazine." Probably very unhappy with their decision to post that picture. "Are you okay? Did Olivia do something again?"

Mom used to be able to pretend she liked Olivia. Now, she only seems to tolerate her. She stays out of my business as much as possible, but it's pretty clear she's not a fan.

LOVE IN B MINOR

"I'm fine."

"See, honey, I told you you were worried about nothing," she tells my dad.

"In one of the pictures, you look so sad. I only wanted to make sure you're doing fine."

"I only saw one picture."

"Oh." Mom sounds like she wishes she could take her word back. But it's too late.

"Mom?" I probe her.

"There are several articles talking about how depressed you are and that yesterday you were letting loose after not finding someone to dance in the music video which is dedicated to Benji."

"How do they know about this video already?" I clench my hands into fists. Stupid Grégoire.

"Anyways, we only wanted to make sure you were doing okay. Are we still seeing you for lunch on Sunday?"

"Of course. I'll be there."

"We love you, honey." And she hangs up. Mom and Dad keep me grounded. I never miss a Sunday lunch unless we're on tour or performing, and I'm

already looking forward to next Sunday. At my parents'
table, nothing is expected of me except setting the table,
and clearing out. Mom and Dad have disagreed with me
a lot in the past years. Even though they supported my
music career, they didn't expect me to not go to college
and to drop everything to tour. Benji's death really hurt
them. He was like another son to them. And Mom
broke down at his funeral.

It's too much at once. The auditions, the stupid
gossip rag playing on Benji's death again, being so
close to Jen but knowing I can't have her.

The sun shines through the windows,
illuminating the keys of the piano. I play for a few more
minutes, losing myself in the music, and then yawn
loudly.

Taking a nap so early in the morning might not
be considered napping, but I don't really care. I stand
up and unfold my wide frame on the couch. And I close
my eyes.

A pounding of my door wakes me up from a
very bizarre dream, where Grégoire was a snake

attempting to eat Jen and me. And we weren't mice or anything.

"Open up!" And the snake is at the door.

"I'm coming. I'm coming!" I drag myself out of bed and unlatch the door. "It's twelve. I'm not late to any appointment and you've got yours soon."

"Look at this." He shoves his iPad into my face.

'What?"

"Read the headline."

"This is ridiculous." I sigh—irritated, but glance down at the headline. "Dancer chosen for Dire Blue new music video. Is she the new Benji?"

Fuck.

CHAPTER 26 – JEN

As soon as I enter the studio, Alisha rushes to me. "I saw the news online. About you know…and you know who. Are you okay?" She looks worried.

"I'm fine. I don't think it's true and even if it was, we're just friends."

"Yeah okay."

"Stop probing or I'm going to talk to you about a certain Steve who's been asking about you."

"He has?" She has the dreamiest look on her face mixed with so much fear.

"He has."

LOVE IN B MINOR

Erin—the dancer who also tried out for the auditions—enters with her head down. When she sees us, a ghost of a smile appears on her face and she walks to us. "How did you guys do yesterday?"

"Hmm-hmmm." That's the best reply I can come up with. Clearly, I'm going to be amazing in interviews if Grégoire decides I need to do any.

"I was a bit distracted, but I did pretty well," Alisha answers. "How about you?"

"I panicked, but like you said, I gathered everything I had and still danced, but the choreography I prepared was too short and it didn't fit the mood of the music. It is such a sad melody."

"True," I reply—keeping the rest of the story inside because it's not my story to tell.

More dancers trickle into the room. Many are talking about the article in *Le Monde* about the dance company. It made a big splash on social media, apparently, and some seem to be anxious about their jobs. "If we don't sell out at the next show, we can forget it. This company has so much debt. They should have been upfront before offering us a position."

217

John—one of the choreographers—enters and goes straight to business like he usually does. He's not as mean as Igor, but he does push us to our limits. "Let's go. Enough of this chitchatting. I have you with me for three hours and you're going to work for three hours. Not talk. Do you hear me?"

Everybody quiets down. "Let's get started."

After three hours, I'm out of breath, my feet are bleeding and my entire body is shaking. John seems pretty pleased with our performance. "I'll let Igor know that you did well today."

It's like throwing us a bone—we're all so eager to please Igor, even though that's Mission Impossible. It's sad in a way how much power ballet directors and choreographers have over us. If they decide we're not good enough, or we didn't do something properly, we don't get a good part, we can get fired, we can be burned on the entire circuit.

I lean toward Alisha. "I need to go to talk to Igor."

"I'm so excited for you." And I believe her.

LOVE IN B MINOR

I drink water, throw on my pants and drag my feet to Igor's office. Audrey smiles at me when I enter the imposing room full of old paintings and pictures of him dancing. "He's waiting for you."

"What?"

"He said if someone gets that audition, he's sure it's going to be Jennifer Harrison."

I don't think I could be more surprised if I tried. Igor has never ever praised me for anything. And he never gave me the impression that he thought I was that good. Some days, I even had to wonder why he allowed me to delay my acceptance into his company, since he always yells at me that I'm not good enough, not talented enough.

"Come on in." His Russian accent is still there, and it's even mixed with a French accent. He's been living in France for the past twenty years, and he calls himself more Parisian than the Parisians. Whatever that means.

I hold the paperwork to my chest, trying not to look intimidated. I shouldn't be. We've all seen Igor lose his temper often enough to sometimes not take him seriously, but his career…his career is impressive. His way of dancing, of transcending emotions, of making everything look oh so easy. That's impressive. Plus, he danced with the most talented, he danced in front of the Queen of England, in front of stars and kings.

"I am guessing you got the part." He leans back in his leather chair. His dark cherry desk is imposing, but what's more imposing is the picture of him and Baryshnikov smiling like old friends.

"I did." I'm waiting for him to tell me to sit down but he simply stares at me. He waits. Like he did when he called me personally to let me know I was offered a position in his ballet company and I explained I could not accept it, that my sister was offered a new trial treatment and we were not sure if it was going to work or not. That I could not leave without knowing I would see her again. Back then, he simply said, "I will call you again in one month. If you cannot take the position before October then I will need to find someone else who can."

His voice didn't sound warm or empathetic or like he felt anything at all. But I was grateful he gave me that extra time. When he called again a month later, we all thought Mia would get better, Mia wanted me to take the position.

His expression softens for only a split second, and maybe I imagined it because his voice is hard when he speaks again. "My sources told me which band it was for."

"Your sources?" I bite my tongue to not laugh out loud. This sounds like an episode of a crime movie.

"I have my connections in the show business too. From my short-lived career in the film industry." He taps his fingers on the desk and bores his eyes into mine. He looks like he's waiting for me to say something, but instead, I take a seat across from him. This staying standing isn't working, and I need to at least pretend like I have control over what I do. Over my own career.

"I think it would be good for me. That it would be good for the company."

"How so?"

"The video is going to air before the show. There's high interest for it. It's the first song ever since…"

"Ever since that boy died of an overdose." Again, his eyes turn soft, cloudy, almost like he has a story of his own. Everyone has a story. And everyone has sadness in their story, even when it ends with a happily ever after. There's always sadness somewhere. And people deal with it in different ways. "I want to make sure it is not going to be detrimental for the image of the company. While I am entertaining the idea of showing ballet in more modern circumstances, like in that music video, to remind people how much emotion one can put in ballet movements, how incredible it is to dance and tell a story, I also want to make sure we do not alienate our regular donors…who are…a bit more classically oriented."

"Okay."

"And so I would like to ask you something. I will say yes no matter what, but maybe we could kill two birds with one stone."

"What do you mean?"

LOVE IN B MINOR

"What if the main singer...Lucas is his name, right? What if he came and performed the song during our show?"

"Didn't you say that it might attract the wrong type of people for the company?"

"Not if he played the melody on the piano and you danced it. Think of it as a solo. A very important solo. Then, we could probably sell out and get amazing coverage in all media. Maybe we could put the video on YouTube and get more viewers." It almost looks like he's talking to himself, reminding himself of his vision for this company, of what he wanted it to become.

"I don't know if he would do it."

Igor leans forward, tilts his head to the side and the smile he has on isn't friendly or enthusiastic, it's calculating, and a chill runs down my spine. "I have a feeling that if you ask him, he will do it."

I shouldn't be surprised by what he said. He's Igor. Well known for his scheming and his manipulating. But still, my eyes widen. "I don't know if he would do it," I repeat. And what I don't say is, "I don't know if I want to ask him."

"We'll discuss this later. For now, here is a paper stating that you are authorized to work on this music video as long as the hours do not interfere with your training at the company. Think about what I said—you may hold the key for the company to survive. And think about all those dancers who will need to find another job. Some would need to go back to their countries. Some might not be able to dance any longer because this was their last stop before retirement."

I nod, stand up and leave the office in a daze. I text Lucas before going back to train. I can't bring myself to ask him about the performance, though. He's already so wary about everything, wondering if everyone is out to use him. *Talked to Igor. He's okay with everything. I'll see you this afternoon.*

And then I replay the entire conversation in my head.

Igor is pretty much telling me I can make or break his company.

No pressure.

CHAPTER 27 - LUCAS

I run my fingers through my hair. This is fucking ridiculous. Grégoire looks beyond pissed, but he also has an "I told you so" smirk on his face that I want to punch away.

He points to his iPad in my hand. "Keep reading."

Coming between Olivia and Lucas, Jennifer Harrison could be the one to prevent the band from getting back together for its memorial song for Benjamin Graves, the band member who died from an overdose last year.

"This is bullshit!" I stride over to the counter and punch it, wincing at the pain that radiates from my hand to my shoulder.

"What is bullshit is that I'm meeting with Fran in thirty minutes and the news is already out. Someone blabbered, and it better not be your new girlfriend."

"She didn't. She went to her company to rehearse for her show and she was going to talk to her director."

"When was she supposed to be done?"

"She was going to talk to him around eleven and tell him not to announce anything. She was going to text me that Igor did agree with it, because of that clause in her contract." I shuffle through my winter coat to find my phone.

There's one text from Jen. *Igor agrees and actually seems happy for the first time ever. I'll see you at the studio at 2 p.m.*

Grégoire plops himself on the couch. "We need to do some damage control. I need a new scoop for Fran, otherwise she's going to start digging and writing shit about you guys."

LOVE IN B MINOR

"I've got nothing to hide."

"Everyone has something to hide." He doesn't look me in the face when he says it, and I'm not sure if he's talking about me or about himself.

"Why don't you just tell Fran about Olivia singing that song with me?"

Grégoire perks up right away. It almost looks like he's happy too. "Really? I thought you wanted to see how it was working before agreeing to it."

"We know we sing well together. We know how to work with each other. We know Benji's grandmother will love it if she can remember who we are." My voice is almost breaking. Every single time I see Benji's grandmother, my chest tightens so much it's almost hard to breathe, but I always pretend to be happy. Right now I'll pretend I'm okay with everything. "I'm over Olivia and it would be good to honor Benji's memory together."

"Plus, it would put to rest all those theories about her and Benji." He pauses. "Are you sure?"

"I'm sure."

"Okay. Then I'm going. I don't want to be late for the lunch, but do me a favor."

"Another one?" I raise an eyebrow in my signature "what the fuck" move.

"Maybe check with your girlfriend that she doesn't talk to anyone about the band without my consent and guidance. It's in her contract. If she messes up, she can kiss any career goodbye."

"Don't be like that." My tone is a warning, but as always, Grégoire only cares about Grégoire.

"And don't be naïve. She's probably after easy fame. Or maybe she wants money." He pauses and smiles—like the snake of my dreams. "Okay fine, she probably doesn't want money, her parents are loaded. Which is a good thing."

"You checked up on her parents?"

"Of course I did. And that story about her sister is heart-wrenching."

"Don't you dare use any of this without talking to her first!"

"You know me. I always play by the rules." He grabs his iPad back and slides out of my apartment, probably sensing I'm two seconds away from exploding.

I grab my phone back. *It seems you're going to get a fast crash course in dealing with shitty gossip. Coming to pick you up. Sorry it's already starting to get out of hand.*

She said this morning she was going to leave rehearsals around 1:30 p.m. She's probably still there—that's why she's not answering.

And part of me worries it's going to be too much for her. She seems to be a private person, she has a hard time talking about her sister, about her past. What is she going to do when people follow her every move, question her every word?

I used to feel bad for even questioning what came with being a performer. I used to believe that everything I did was fair game for public consumption. But it's not. My life is still my life. I'm an entertainer, and I'm grateful, but I don't owe the entire world an insight into my thoughts.

Last year before everything went down to shit, Olivia's naked pictures were stolen from her phone.

Pictures she sent me. Pictures that were only meant for the both of us. She sobbed in my arms, as the pictures wound up on thousands of websites with people commenting on how hot or ugly she was, how they wanted her, or how she was a slut. Seeing her so destroyed, seeing how she couldn't stop thinking about it every single time someone looked at her in a certain way or snickered, seeing how she couldn't sleep, anger crushed into me. I hurt for her.

That's when Olivia decided to take control of her own publicity in a sense. Seeing those pictures of herself spread everywhere, she realized her life didn't only belong to herself anymore, and that was tough.

How is Jen going to react?

I stare at my screen. But still no answer.

I check the time. One. If I call my driver now, I could make it to her ballet company when she's done, bring her back to her place and then drive her to the studio.

It's funny and scary how much I care already.

CHAPTER 28 – JEN

The rehearsals are running late. "One more time," John repeats, and I'd rather he would yell because this cold voice without intonation is usually a sign he's really unhappy with us. And when John is angry, he's almost as bad as Igor.

"Grace! Your turnout is so wrong I don't even know how you could call yourself a dancer!" Grace tries harder—she's one of the oldest here. She told me the other day that this company is her last hurrah, one more way to show that you can be forty and still dance professionally. She was a star dancer in the San Diego

Ballet Company, but John doesn't seem to care about her past right now. He's all about business. "Come on, Grace! If you wince like this, do you think anybody is going to believe you? I don't know what Igor was thinking when he accepted you."

Grace huffs but she doesn't answer. Instead, she tries harder.

"Alex…you need to bring Alisha higher, much higher. And Alisha, maybe you should try pretending you know what you're doing once in a while."

Alex curses under his breath and Alisha blushes, but they continue.

John walks past me and I expect him to scold me. I don't expect him to yell into my ear. I almost lose my balance. "This is not an arabesque. This is a joke of an arabesque!" He pulls on my leg, but I don't move. My entire muscles are tensed the way they're supposed to be. "You look like the Pisa Tower, your balance is barely there." He leans his head back and stares up at the ceiling. "This is ridiculous. I'm supposed to prep you for one of the biggest shows of this ballet company, and this is what I have to work with? A bunch of amateurs!" He walks past Erin and looks her up and down like he's looking at a piece of meat. I can see them in the mirror, the way she stares back at him without blinking.

"Sergei was fired for a reason," she says loud enough for everybody to hear, and silence falls onto the studio. Erin did not stutter, she did not hesitate. John clears his throat and moves on to the next person.

Sergei was fired three weeks ago. The rumor goes that he was being way too friendly with the dancers in exchange for bigger and better roles.

Igor said he wouldn't have any of this in his company. It wasn't about spreading your legs but about talent. His words, not mine.

I smile at Erin in the mirror and see her chest rising and falling. She was bluffing, she looks petrified now, but I discreetly give her a thumbs-up. Because she did it, standing up for herself without hesitation.

"Okay, fine, you can go! I'll see some of you later this afternoon." He dismisses us and stares right ahead as he exits the room.

"That was pretty impressive, Erin," I tell her after shaking my muscles. Everything hurts, and I don't even know if an ice bath is going to enable me to move again after holding several positions for longer than was required.

"A friend of mine left the company because of what happened with Sergei. She's still not over it, and seeing her so lost…I got mad when I saw the way he was looking at me. The way he told me he could help me if I wanted."

"He said what?"

"He leaned in and whispered it to me. I'm going to mention it to Audrey…but I don't think they'll fire him. They can't keep on firing people. And he didn't *do* anything." And she sighs, because she may be right. And it's not fair.

"What time is it?" I ask, changing the topic when I realize I might be late for my first production meeting.

Erin shuffles through her shoulder bag and turn on her phone. "One forty-five," Erin answers and then her eyes widen. She opens her mouth. "You made it."

LOVE IN B MINOR

"What?"

She shows me her phone. She received a text from her sister telling her I got the part. "That's you. You made it into the video." She jumps and hugs me and I don't have time to react before the rest of the room explodes in chatter. It seems Grégoire released the information earlier than planned.

I gather my stuff quickly, turn my phone back on. We can't have our phones on during rehearsal unless we want to face the wrath of the entire crew.

There are hundreds of notifications from Twitter and Facebook and Instagram. The last time I posted anything was last month. It doesn't make sense. My mailbox is full and there are also hundreds of text messages. Hundreds of messages of love and hate from total strangers. "What the heck is going on?"

Alisha turns to me, her mouth wide open. "It's out. People know you got the part…and…"

"And what?"

I scroll down to one message which has been sent at least fifty times. *Why don't you go and die, you ugly bitch? He's never going to want to be with you. He's mine. Only mine.*

Wow. That's encouraging.

Alisha shows me her phone. "And your name, your phone number have been posted online." My mouth gapes open and I stare at her screen. My cell phone number is on some random blog and that post has already been retweeted four thousand times.

Some of the other dancers gather around us. "Hey Jen, congrats!" Then another takes a picture of me. "You're going on my Instagram. I can't believe you know Lucas."

"Okay, calm down." Igor enters the room. But even he can't stop the effervescence that has taken over. "I said, calm down!"

I snap out of my stupor and with shaking fingers, I scroll down my text messages until I see one from Lucas. *It seems you're going to get a fast crash course in dealing with shitty gossip. Coming to pick you up. Sorry it's already starting to get out of hand.*

What is everyone talking about?

And then Alisha gently shows me her phone.

LOVE IN B MINOR

And I see the picture, and the headlines, and my phone beeps again with another hate message, and my throat tightens until it's hard to breathe.

CHAPTER 29 – LUCAS

There is a small crowd forming outside. And they're waiting for her. They're already trying to dissect her. Olivia almost broke down, she lost a part of herself. How is Jen going to react?

How is she going to deal with everything?

I text Grégoire. *Do you have the number of the ballet company director?*

Why?

I need to talk to him. See if there's a back entrance or another way into the building. It's not too bad yet, but I want to talk to Jen before she gets into this craziness.

Good idea. I don't think she's equipped yet to deal with that by herself.

He texts me Igor Baraski's number and I call him, arranging that Jen will exit via the garden they have and not via the courtyard. I tell my driver to turn around, grateful nobody has noticed the Peugeot we're using.

As soon as we pull over, Jen shows up. She looks bewildered. It's not in the way she walks because she still looks like she owns the room. And I'm sure anyone else who saw her right now would think she has it all together, but I know better. She's playing with her hair, and her mouth is pursed into a thin line. She hugs her friend Alisha. And I open the passenger door. She slides in and her hands shake slightly as she puts them on her knees.

"Did you see the article?"

"They got my number. I don't know how, but they got my number." She swallows her tears. "I was fine, you know, death threats and stuff but whatever.

People are going to be haters, right?" Her shoulders now tremble the same way as her hands, and she pulls out her cell phone.

Her voice drops to a whisper. "Look what they wrote, how can someone write something like this?"

Ur r such an aful personn. Y let ur sister dy.

The anger that was simmering below the surface is boiling and I punch the seat in front of me, wrap my arm around her and pull her close to me. "I'm sorry. I'm so sorry."

"I don't understand. Attacking me is one thing, but talking about my sister?" She sniffles and buries her head into my shoulder, taking a deep breath like she's trying to regain control. "I need to call my parents, I need to tell them what's going on so they don't hear about it from someone else."

But her phone rings before she can dial the number. "Do you know this number?" I ask her and she shakes her head. "I don't know that many people in France, and that's a French number." I send it to voice mail and turn off her cell. "We'll get you a new number. Why don't you use my cell to call your parents?"

She nods and sits further away from me as she dials. "Mom?" Her voice is firmer, like she wants to pretend she's okay even though she's clearly shaken. Who wouldn't be?

"I'm okay. Yes, I'm sorry. I should have called you and let you know I got the part. I'm so sorry."

She listens to whatever her mom is saying and then she closes her eyes. "Yes, Dad. I'm sure. No, I don't want to go home. I'm doing this. It's going to help me, and the company, and Dad, Mia wouldn't want me to give up. She wouldn't want me to give up," she repeats and this time I believe she's calmer. As if thinking about her sister is giving her new strength. I touch her knee and when she hangs up, she puts her hand on mine, interlinking our fingers. It calms me too.

"What did they say?"

"Someone got their home number too. We're not even listed. They received phone calls early this morning and they've been trying to reach me, but I turned off my phone until I finished rehearsing. I didn't realize how mean people can be." She forces her lips into a smile that looks so sad, I want to envelop into my arms again. "And I used to be a mean girl."

"What do you mean?"

"When my sister got diagnosed, I had…issues. And I don't know, I turned myself into a mean girl to protect myself. Kids used to say the meanest things to me when I first started at the School of Performing Arts, and I decided to turn the tables on them."

"Attack before you get hit?"

"Pretty much. But it got to be a bit too much—I took my role a bit too much to heart. I got better though."

"Are you really sure you want to go through with this?"

"I am. I need to change my number but it has to calm down, right?"

"I'm sure it will. The thing is that people got so angry when we stopped playing after Benji died, Olivia and I split up, we canceled concert after concert. At the beginning, fans were understanding, but then it got a bit crazy. We were losing our audience. This is our comeback, so the scrutiny is intense.'

"Did Grégoire talk to that blogger lady earlier than planned? I don't understand."

"Apparently, someone else leaked it." And I glance at her. She's leaning against the seat. Her hair is all over the place. She didn't do it.

"Why?" She sounds genuinely surprised. "I don't get it. Why leak it?"

"People like to have good relationships with influential bloggers or journalists—it gives them a sense of importance or it helps them sabotage others."

"Wow, that sounds like fun. Not." She shakes her head and takes her hand away from mine. "I need to go and take a shower before the meeting, I need to go back home and grab other clothes in case the shooting director already wants me to dance."

"Your place might be crowded. Do you have more clothes in your bag?"

"I have the clothes I went into the school with this morning: baggy pants and a sweater."

"Those baggy pants look good on you." I try to joke but it falls flat when she keeps on staring ahead. "Why don't you come back to my place, take a shower and then we'll head out to the studio. Today is all about reading the script and about Olivia and I singing that song together to see if it still fits what the director had in mind."

"I don't want to bother you."

"Are you kidding me? You won't bother me at all." And then because I want to see a smile in her eyes again. Because I want to make sure she understands I'm there for her. And because I want to believe we might stand a chance in the future, I say, "We're friends after all, right?"

When a smile forms on her lips, I'm tempted to cradle her face in my hands and taste her mouth again, but instead I only offer my hand. She stares at it for a second before linking our fingers together again.

"Right."

"Take us to the Eiffel apartment," I tell Matthieu, our driver.

LOVE IN B MINOR

"We'll be there in ten minutes," he replies.

Drivers are always so discreet you almost forget they're there, but for a second I look at him from the mirror.

Everyone becomes suspicious when you don't know where the possible leaks come from.

CHAPTER 30 – JEN

His apartment looks the same and oh so different. Every turn reminds me of that night we spent together. The counter against which he kissed me. The oven where he baked the cookies. The way I licked the dough from his fingers.

That shower might need to be cold. It's funny how my mind tries so hard to focus on something other than the pain I feel deep in my chest.

I still can't believe someone would bring Mia into the mix.

LOVE IN B MINOR

Lucas hands me a towel and his eyes darken, his mouth opens slightly and he rubs the back of his neck. His voice sounds gruffer when he speaks again. "There…I'll be waiting. I texted Grégoire that we'll be a tad late but that we'll be there as soon as possible."

I know he's feeling it too, the pull between us, the air crackling, full of delicious tension. For a split second, I'm tempted to forget everything, to use him to forget everything, to drop my towel and throw myself into his arms. By the look of him, he wouldn't push me away.

But it's not fair. Not fair to him and not fair to me. I can't keep on repeating the mistakes of my past. That's what my therapist told me once, that I needed to break the cycle. And yes, I still stumbled along the way, but I want to believe that I'm out of the darker path.

"Thank you." I turn away and hurry into the bathroom. There's something intimate about showering in a guy's place. Like we're an item, like it's our life, like we want to spend as much time together as possible.

His bathroom is super clean—and I may or may not carefully take his cologne bottle and sniff it. It's him. I'm tempted to find a piece of paper I could spray it on and keep with me, but clearly that's the crushing part of my brain talking. Because that's not what friends do. Friends don't think about opening the door and asking their friend to come join them in the shower.

I turn on the shower, take off my clothes and wait until it's at least a bit warm before stepping in. My mind turns and turns but it always comes back to two important facts: one, I should tell him about what I did, and soon; and two, I really *really* like him.

CHAPTER 31 – LUCAS

The sound of the water tempts me. If the water is running, she's in the shower and if she's in the shower, I could massage the tension away from her shoulders, I could kiss every inch of her skin. But I can't just go and knock on the door and ask her if she needs help showering. That sounds way too cheesy, and she made it clear so many times that she only wants to be friends.

So instead of giving in to my desires, I sit down at my computer and try to do some damage control. I haven't been on social media since the band split up, but I still lurk from time to time. My last tweet was from January last year.

Thanks everyone for the love and support. Need some time to regroup. Talk later.

That tweet had so many notifications that I stopped checking.

I clear my throat and cross my fingers Grégoire is not going to go via the deep end. He must have already told that woman about Olivia because the first tweets are coming in my feed. "Oh wow, the band is reuniting!"

"Olivia and Lucas Forever."

"Fuck Olivia."

Fuck that Jen girl."

People really tend to forget themselves behind a screen. I crack my knuckles and type. "New song. New video. It's going to be awesome." No hashtag because I can't think of any, but I do tag Olivia in it. Trying to leave Jen out of the spotlight as much as possible.

And then I call Grégoire. "Jen needs a new number. Can someone take care of that?"

LOVE IN B MINOR

"How is she doing?" And he actually sounds genuinely worried.

"Like shit. People were attacking her from all sides."

"I'm almost at your door. Your driver said he dropped you off at your apartment, right?"

"You don't need to come here."

"Actually, I do. I talked with the director of her ballet company, and both of them came up with a great idea to promote both the new song and their company. Jen is much shrewder than I gave her credit for."

And my hands clam up, the same old doubts come crashing back. "What do you mean, she came up with a new idea?"

"Let's talk once I'm there."

I totally forgot to tell Grégoire about what I put up on Twitter and how I want to try to drive the narrative. My eyes dart back to the bathroom door. The water has stopped. Why would Jen talk about a possible marketing idea with her ballet company first? Why didn't she come to me?

Everyone has an agenda. Everyone is always looking for something more. Olivia's words come back to haunt me. After I confronted her about sharing those pictures of us, about giving an interview about Benji, about the fake engagement, she looked up at me, her eyes full of tears. And that's what she told me. Then, she said, "And you're looking for someone who is not me. That's why I left the band. I thought maybe you'd chase after me. But you didn't."

"I never used you!"

"Of course you did. We used each other and that's why we're so broken now. I'm sorry for everything. I really am. But I'm not the only one to blame."

Was she right?

Did I use her in some way?

I loved her. I did. I never betrayed her the way she did with me. I could have forgiven the engagement story if she had come clean with it. Our trip to Corsica two weeks after Benji died was supposed to get us back on track; it was our last chance to save a relationship that had felt like it was way past its expiration date. I had lingering doubts about her and Benji. I didn't want to believe the gossip magazines, but she lied so many times.

And if I'm a hundred percent honest with myself, I still had doubts nothing happened between her and Benji while I was giving interviews in the UK for several weeks.

Jen opens the door from the bathroom, her hair in a knot above her head. She's back in her sweatpants and sweater from the School of Performing Arts. She looks so fragile yet so strong. And with her I have a feeling I've never really had with Olivia. With her, I feel like we could support one another, lean on each other. That there wouldn't only be one taking and the other giving.

"Hey... Can I talk to you?' she asks and plops herself next to me on the couch. She smells like my shower gel.

"Of course. Is it about what you and your director came up with to do more marketing?"

She raises one eyebrow in the way I've learned she sometimes shows she's confused. "What are you talking about?" She leans back and crosses her leg under her. She looks so at ease, so much like she belongs, and it's hard to keep my thoughts straight.

"Grégoire is coming over. He mentioned you and your director thought about a special event to help promote both your company and the new song."

"Ohhh...I didn't suggest anything. My director apparently has some sources who told him what band was auditioning, and he had the idea that during the show we have next month, you come and play the piano while I dance."

The expression on her face remains open, like she's telling the truth. "Okay," I say slowly.

"But there's something else I need to tell you. And I need to tell it to you before Grégoire arrives."

"What?"

"It's about..." The doorbell rings but she puts her hand on my arm.

"Please, you've got to listen to me. I don't want you to hear about it from anyone else."

LOVE IN B MINOR

I ignore the doorbell; my entire attention is on her, on the way she bites her lip and on the way she looks so distressed I want to take her in my arms.

"I…I had a problem with drugs."

My mouth opens but there's no sound. I shake my head. The doorbell continues ringing and I stride to the door. "Grégoire, give us two minutes. Okay? Two minutes."

And I turn back to her. She squares her shoulders like she's ready for a fight.

CHAPTER 32 – JEN

I wanted to wait until I saw my new therapist. I wanted to wait until I could make sense of all my feelings, but I can't wait. Because if I wait, I might hurt him even more, and that's not fair.

He stares at me and for the first time, I can't decipher his expression. "I used drugs," I repeat and even though my voice is somewhat steady, my insides are shaking. I expect him to yell or to ask me to leave. Not to sit back down and to force himself to calm down, which I know he's doing by the way he's breathing in and out.

LOVE IN B MINOR

"When?" His tone is even.

The words are hard to come out, but they do. Slowly, painfully.

His cell phone continues to ring, but Lucas ignores it. "Don't worry about." His voice is calm and almost soothing even though his face doesn't reveal anything about his feelings.

So I continue talking through the doorbell and the phone calls. Grégoire must be losing it. I tell Lucas about the shame and the tears, about the stay in the rehab center, about my therapy, about my coping mechanisms. I'm not hiding anything anymore.

"Why did you tell me?"

"I wanted to…I didn't want you to find out from one of those gossip reporters or anyone else. I wanted to be the one to tell you."

"But why?"

I struggle to answer. Because the reason I wanted to tell him myself is for him to really know me, to know the good and the bad, to make him understand that I trust him. And that I want him to trust me. Because I don't want to hurt him in any way.

"Why?" he asks again—his breath tickles my neck, and I didn't even realize I had closed my eyes. When I open them, he's closer to me. His hand reaches my face and he caresses it. "You could have made up something. You could have lied—saying it wasn't true. That you were used."

I lean into his hand, letting his warmth spread through me. "Because…because I was scared to hurt you…if you found out any other way. And at first I was afraid to tell you because I was scared you would look at me differently."

"I understand everything about making mistakes. And learning from them. You made a mistake. You almost died. Yes, I would have been pissed if you never told me about it, but I'm also pissed you felt like you had to hide it from me in the first place. Not pissed at you. At me."

And he sounds so much like that first night we spent together. And because I've been fighting my feelings for what seems like forever even though I've known him for such a short time, and because I feel a connection I've never felt before with someone, I lean in and kiss him.

He seems surprised at first, but only for a second. "Finally," he whispers and pulls me closer to him. His mouth is urgent, and passionate, and I want more. I want everything. I want him.

Someone must have opened to Grégoire because there are loud knocks at Lucas' door. He yells, "You better be dressed and ready to go!" He sounds pissed, but it might be more efficient if he didn't sound pissed half of the time.

"We need to tell him about all of this. Before more things are spread everywhere…."

CHAPTER 33 - LUCAS

Jen tenses at my words, and I want to find a way to reassure her it's going to be okay, but I don't know for sure. Benji's death showed me the uncertainty of it all. The uncertainty about life and friendships and dreams.

Grégoire knocks again and this time, I get up—after kissing Jen slightly on the cheek. It's a reassuring kiss, but her smile is still tense.

"What took you so long?" He barges in like he owns the place. Like he usually does. And then his eyes dance past me, land on Jen, who's now sitting straight on the couch.

LOVE IN B MINOR

"And here I thought you two could actually keep your hands off each other. It is a bad idea. A very bad idea." He pauses and shakes his head in his 'I think you're losing it" way. He glares at me. "I did tell you that you two shouldn't even think about starting whatever it is you're starting. And if it's a booty call you want, you can have that with pretty much anybody out there."

I raise my hand to stop him and step forward. My voice is low, a warning. "Don't continue in that direction. You can talk to us about what you think is appropriate while we work together, but don't you dare minimize what we have."

"What you have? You've been together for what, a whole five seconds? Come on, it's lust at his best."

"Shut up or get out."

Our staring contest is full of unsaid words. Like, why didn't he pay more attention to Benji? Even though I shouldn't blame him for what happened, it's easier to find a way out than to beat myself up all the time. Neither of us backs down until Jen calls my name. "Let's talk about something else, shall we?"

She sounds calm, but her eyes betray how worried she is.

"Jen is right." Grégoire gives in and I gesture for them to sit at the table.

"We need to tell him too, don't we?" Jen asks me in the cold voice I know is her way of protecting herself. I take her hand in mine, a way to make sure she knows I'm standing with her.

"What? You're pregnant? Already?" Grégoire's joke falls flat.

Jen flinches and tightens her grip on mine.

I force my body to stay relaxed. Punching Grégoire would only give me temporary release. Nothing more. "Shut up, Grégoire. Jen told me about something that happened several years ago and that she thinks people could dig out." I tell him the story and fully expect him to go ballistic. When he found out Olivia was spreading rumors about us being engaged, he lost it. He totally lost it.

LOVE IN B MINOR

But now, he's staying pretty composed. "We can use this. It's actually kind of perfect."

"Perfect?" Jen voices my surprise in a much more nuanced way than I would.

"We can say this has been planned from the very beginning. That Lucas knew of your past and that the song was a reminder of what you fought against. It gives us even more meat on why he chose you." He raises his index finger up the air. "That's what we're going to do, we'll say there were two dancers very close to getting the part and that you were chosen because of your connection." He stares at Lucas. "A much better reason than you wanting to get into her pants. Way less dangerous."

I whistle—for once impressed with his way of handling things—but I need to check with Jen. I need to make sure she's okay with all of this. If she wants to stop and not go on with the video, I'd understand. "What do you think?"

"I actually think it could work. And let's face it, I probably will have a much more personal way of listening to the song than other people."

"Are you sure you want to go through with this? We could pull the plug." I ignore Grégoire's protest. "You say the word and we can change the concept. I wouldn't want any other dancers than you, but it's your choice."

"I'm sure. I told you." Her smile doesn't reach her eyes, and for one second I want to ask her again why she's so set on doing this video, why it's so important to her, not able to shake the feeling she needs it more than she admitted. She continues, "I think it's time for me to show that I've really grown out of my addiction I will need to call Igor, the director of the company. He's probably not going to be pleased by this entire story. He was worried about more drug stories involving company dancers getting to the press."

"I'll handle him" Grégoire stands up. "By the way, Lucas, I saw you're back on Twitter. Your fans will be pleased. Good job. Now let's get moving. We have a video to make, and I do want to remind you both to keep whatever you have under wraps. We're not dealing with this story right now. I told you I don't want any love triangle stories. So, keep it quiet. Best would be to nip it in the bud, but I have a feeling you won't listen."

"I can do what I want," I protest, but Jen reaches out to me.

She leans in toward me and purses her lips. She seems to do that whenever she's doing something she doesn't really want to do, but she knows it's right. "Between the drugs story coming out and all the crap you're already dealing with... Let's wait. We'll do the friends part first like we said, and as soon as the video and my show is over, we can see where this is going."

I groan, frustrated on so many levels, but I know she's right. Starting a relationship right under the spotlight is also not the best way to get to know someone without any pressure.

"Okay, let's go. We're going to be late, and the director of that music video is very big on punctuality. Not sure if it's because he's German or the best in his job, but he won't appreciate it if we're late."

Grégoire stands up and I push him out. "Give us two seconds."

I close the door on his bewildered face.

"What are you doing?"

"Friends first? Are you sure?" I'm dying to kiss her again, to dig my fingers into her hair, to pull her to me.

She bites her upper lip, glances down and then back at me, hesitating. "I told you another reason I wanted to stay friends was because I didn't think you and Olivia were entirely done. To be honest, this time as friends will tell me if…"

"Why can't you just believe me when I'm telling you it's over?" I want to wrap my arms around her but I stay put.

"Because of the way you keep on looking at her, like the hurt you're feeling may be covering more than a feeling of betrayal. We can't start fresh if you're still reeling from your past relationship. Trust me."

"You're being way too reasonable."

"I have my moments." She opens the door and pulls me outside with her. "Come on, let's go before my not-so-reasonable brain takes over. Let's get started on this video."

LOVE IN B MINOR

And I hope that for once I'm not making a mistake in trusting someone.

CHAPTER 34 - JEN

In the car driving us to the studio, I turn on my phone for only a second to text my parents so they know there might soon be stories about my incident in Cape Cod. I don't read any other text messages, because reading about hate and people wanting to see me die isn't exactly a mood booster.

Mom calls me right back and I manage to calm her down, promising her that everything will be fine. I make a mental note to call Emilia as soon as I'm back in my apartment to give her the news first.

LOVE IN B MINOR

The car pulls in front of a big modern building in La Défense neighborhood. My eyes scan all the details: the big bay windows, the long elevators, the plants and flowers at every corner. It smells like air freshener and roses, an interesting mix. The receptionist has a warm smile, and everyone around us looks very professional in their business suits, carrying briefcases.

"I'm still wearing my sweatpants." I tug on Lucas' sleeve, sounding maybe a bit more desperate than necessary considering everything else we've been going through.

"You look great, kind of like you planned to wear this," he whispers back and takes my hand in his. I hold on to him. We are rushed to the twenty-eighth floor. Olivia, Steve and Dimitri are already there. Olivia is dressed in what I recognize to be a Stella McCartney pullover black dress. Mom loves that designer and has taken me to several of her shows. The sleeves are long but the front is revealing and hugs her curves. It's supposed to look casual, but really, it is sexy and elegant. Her fiery red hair floats around her, contrasting with the colors of her clothing. She pretty much could grace the cover of *Vogue*, while I could pose for Kohl's.

Which is fine. Because I love Kohl's.

"Hi," Olivia says in a way that makes it clear she knows I've been staring. "It's nice seeing you again."

Steve's smile is warm and kind, and he gives me a nod as if he was welcoming me into their group.

I'm usually not awkward. That's a lie. I am usually awkward, but I'm a pro at hiding it. Now? Not so much. I don't know if I should shake their hands, or maybe give them each a hug. No, definitely not a hug.

Dimitri waves at me, but it's distant, like he's still gauging who I am. He seems to be the silent, brooding type. It must be hard to lose a friend, and a band through no fault of your own.

Steve gives me a fist bump, settling the awkwardness. "So sorry about all the drama already. Welcome to the show business!" Then he dazzles me with a big smile.

"He wants to ask you something," Lucas warns me.

LOVE IN B MINOR

"I haven't talked to Alisha yet," I whisper and Steve's shoulders slouch.

"I get it. But you will, right?"

"I'll mention how wonderful you are, but then it's between her and you—and now tell me, why exactly am I telling her you're wonderful?"

"I'm a decent guy. I work hard. I'm pretty talented. I care about people. I collect stamps."

"Stamps?"

"Yes, stamps. It started when I was eight years old and my family was getting letters from Italy." He shrugs but can't hide his excitement, and I'm not sure I've seen anything cuter than a big sexy guy who's so into something like ...stamps. "Oh, and I also graduated one year early and I'm an engineer by training."

"What kind of engineer?" I tease him.

"Chemical engineer, of course. Those are the best engineers. Really."

Dimitri joins in the conversation. "Don't get him started on his studies. He will never shut up."

"What do you do in your spare time?" I ask Dimitri, thankful for them keeping me busy, so I don't have to look at Olivia talking to Lucas.

"I'm married. I've got two kids." He tilts his head to the side. "I'm a bit older than those two." He pauses and glances at Lucas. "That's why Grégoire is pushing Lucas to be the bad boy of the band. Steve is too outgoing. He wears his heart on his sleeve. People love him but Lucas has the mysterious factor. I'm the one women want to settle down with…" His smile is crooked but warm and sincere.

"How did you get into the band?" I ask him, all curious.

"When the three of them started up, they were missing a drummer. My band had just broken up and Grégoire asked me to join. I love Lucas' way of music and Benji was…he was a genius. Too bad he didn't recognize it himself."

They sound like a family. A family with issues, granted. But a family nonetheless.

And Grégoire claps his hands in a very teacher-trying-to-get everyone's-attention way. "Fabian will be

here very soon. When he gets here, we'll first get to one
of the studios because he has to listen to Olivia and
Lucas singing together. We'll introduce him to Jen and
explain what we've decided to do about the drugs-
related issues she brings with her." He sounds so
dismissive of my past—like it's only a trace of ink in a
long book. But even though I hope he's right, my eyes
still dart to the rest of the group. Steve's and Dimitri's
mouths gape open for a split second while Olivia stares
at me, and I'm not quite sure what is in her eyes. She
whispers something to Lucas, who shakes his head but
doesn't look my way. So maybe it's not about me.

"Hallo, Guten Tag." A man—lanky and tall—
enters the room. He's dressed in jeans and a pullover.
Casual. But definitely not as casual as my sweatpants
and sweater. If he thinks I'm not really looking like the
ballerina he imagined, his eyes don't betray it. "You
must be Jen." He goes straight to me and holds his hand
out. "Igor called me to let me know you've got the
part…and then I saw it on the news."

Igor. Could Igor have told everyone before
Grégoire? I wouldn't put it past him. "Igor and I go way

back. I was assistant director on the movie he starred in back in the eighties. Ancient, I tell you." His German accent is very strong, but he sounds very friendly. I don't know what to say. It's all very surreal, very different than what I expected.

"Hi." This is my witty comeback. I glance at Lucas, who is staring at me, stifling a laugh. I must look quite dumfounded. I close my mouth. And then open it again. "It's very nice meeting you."

"Ja, ja." He turns around to the rest of the group. "We have lots of work to do for this video to be released as soon as you want. I've only read the lyrics, but I want to hear you sing it. I understand Lucas and Olivia are reuniting for this song."

Olivia nods, doesn't say a word. She stays in the back. Carefully watching everyone, including me. She's clearly comfortable in this type of situation. Not like me. And I thought I could fake everything.

"We are singing this song together." Lucas brushes past me and my heart jumps up and down and it's almost like he wants to make sure I know he's thinking about me. This friendship clause I also put on our time together is going to be much harder than I thought. But I need to see this through. Not jump headfirst into a relationship that could break me. And then what? My career also fizzles out? Because let's face it, if anything goes wrong right now, I'm putting my career and the company at risk.

"Okay, then let's go." Fabian guides us through the hallways full of recording trophies and platinum discs, of pictures of him with various artists. I stop in front of an older picture.

"Is that Igor?" I point to the man with long hair wearing elephant jeans. Much different than the one wearing Cartier or Versace pressed costumes who is always so proper.

"Igor was very big on the revolution at the time. He didn't like the conformity of ballet."

"There's not a lot of articles about this."

"He doesn't brag about it either. And he kind of redeemed himself when he joined the Opéra de Paris. He did it to be closer to Audrey, but I don't think they ever got married or even together," Fabian explains, taking his time.

"Audrey Solane?" That would explain why they're so close to one another, but not why they never got married.

"That's her. She was so beautiful. But she was always so scared of letting Igor in. Scared that he would hurt her, not realizing that sometimes letting people in is also another way to love yourself, to give yourself a chance." His voice drops and it's like he's only talking to me. He continues to walk and his words resonate in my mind. Am I being too scared of getting hurt again? Is it too easy to keep Lucas at arm's length because of how stupid and sad I felt when I realized what I wanted from Nick was only a figment of my imagination?

"I'm a big romantic." He laughs louder this time and the entire group turns to us. "People don't think German can be romantics, but have you ever read Heinrich Heine, or this poem by Goethe?" His voice booms and people poke their heads out of their offices with a smile, like it's perfectly normal for him to be reciting German poems in the middle of the day.

" *Ich höre dich,*

   wenn dort mit dumpfem Rauschen

LOVE IN B MINOR

Die Welle steigt.

Im stillen Haine geh' ich oft zu lauschen,

Wenn alles schweigt.'

"Does anyone know what it means?"

Olivia turns to him and with a wistful smile, she

answers. "I hear you,

> when with a dull roar

The wave surges.

In the quiet grove I often go to listen

When all is silent."

"Very good," he replies. Only he and Lucas do

not look surprised. Everyone else stares at Olivia like

they don't know who she is. "I've heard you read and

understand German."

"I do. Not very well, but when I learned how to

sing, I wanted to learn poems from all countries to

maybe get inspiration…I don't know." She glances at

Lucas and their eyes lock for a second too long. Like

they're reminiscing about a memory only the two of

them share, which is probably the case. And there's a sharp pang in my heart.

And I need a second to put my blank mask on again. I force a smile and hurry to walk close to Steve and Dimitri, leaving Olivia and Lucas and my aching heart behind.

Except I can't escape when they're both in the studio singing. I've never heard these lyrics before. During the audition, it was only the melody, the piano mixed with the guitar and the drums.

Right here, right now, it's the both of them…singing together, looking at each other for cues. And while it takes them a while to get comfortable, once they are you see how much they know one another.

And then there are the lyrics. Lyrics so heartbreaking that I wish I could reach out through the glass and touch Lucas, to let him know I'm here. Even though it hurts to see him and Olivia so close to one another, I know how important it is for both of them to grieve.

LOVE IN B MINOR

You...you didn't know how much you meant to us.

You let her take you away. Or did we not see it, did we let it happen?

The guilt eats us away but I'd have a thousand time more pain if it meant seeing you again.

We remember you. Every day. Every day you're part of us.

A light, a sound, a memory that makes us laugh.

Do you remember the time you jumped off a cliff into the water?

Is that where you are now? Jumping cliffs. Jumping into the water?

Little by little you disappeared. She took you. Your spirit, your mind, your hope.

Why didn't you tell me?

"I'm sorry," Olivia says and the tears she seemed to be holding back fall down. Lucas looks like he's not sure what he should do, but then he takes her hand in hers.

Grégoire stands next to me. "They have so much history together."

Steve jumps in, bumping his hip to mine, maybe in a sign of solidarity. "History, yes. Future? I don't think so. Lucas has moved on."

"I'm not so sure. A lot of what happened was emotions running high. That proposal bogus story was a mistake, but the engagement story was not something Olivia planned. I'm sure of that. Someone overheard her talking to a friend and then printed the story. And when she tried her solo career after Benji died, it was also a call for help. She needed him and he didn't see it. She's been trying to convince him, and maybe time spent together is what they need."

"What's in it for you?" Steve sounds angry on my behalf while all I can do is watch Lucas comfort Olivia. Or Olivia comfort Lucas. And pretend that my heart isn't plummeting to the floor, that my heart isn't slowly breaking, that my heart isn't crying along with them.

LOVE IN B MINOR

"Nothing. Except maybe getting my band back together. Those two singing together is such a better show than Lucas alone."

Fabian presses a button, stopping our conversation. "This was great. I think the mood and feelings you're bringing into the song will go nicely with what I have planned for the music video." He pauses and turns to me. He stands taller, more in charge, and I see now the famous producer he is. "Let's go to the meeting room so I can show you my vision."

And as we leave the room, Olivia and Lucas follow closely. I force myself not to look back, not to listen to what Olivia is saying, but I can't help but overhear her telling Lucas: "I've been so lost without you. I understand that you moved on, but you can't deny we still have something."

I hurry closer to Fabian, pretending to ask questions about what is about to happen, how the music video shoot is going to work, what choreographer I'm going to work with.

"So many questions," he replies with a soft turn to his lips. "But I don't think that's really what you're asking yourself, and I have no answers for those ones." He pauses. "But he might." And he strides ahead into the meeting room.

"Hey." Lucas gently puts his hand on my arm and everyone passes in front of us, enters the meeting room, until we're alone in the hallway.

"Hey," I reply but my eyes stay glued to the floor. I don't have any right to be angry and I'm not, but the sadness I feel is almost too much. I miss the time I decided to keep everyone away. I almost regret the promise I made to my sister. And then I hate myself for even thinking this. My mind is racing.

"Would you go somewhere with me after we go through the script?"

"I don't know. I need to be at the ballet company pretty early. Still need to get a new phone number. And I'm kind of scared of what's going to happen once we reveal…" I struggle to find the words. "My past."

"It will only take two hours. I wanted to show you Paris a different way. I promise it's going to be fun.

LOVE IN B MINOR

We could forget about what's going on for a while, go back to that one night."

This time, I look up. "See, that's the thing. We can't simply go back and pretend reality isn't happening. I can't live in a fantasy." My tone is harsh, but he needs to realize that even a friendship can't work if we don't face our issues.

"I get it." He leans in closer to me, too close, way too close for my heart to not try to reach out to his. "Please. One evening, as friends. We won't avoid reality, I promise. But we'll also make sure we find ways to enjoy reality. It's not all darkness and sadness."

And for him to say this while he's hurting moves me, and I nod. "Okay, this evening."

He opens the door for me and I slide in. The band stands in front of a man who isn't as tall as Steve or Dimitri, so I can't see him. But his voice? His voice I recognize.

"Hi Jen. Hope you're ready to work." Igor marches through the small crowd and sits next to Fabian. "I'm happy to be working with you on that choreography."

CHAPTER 35 - LUCAS

Jen seems taken aback by the guy sitting next to Fabian. "Hi, I'm Lucas." I extend my hand to him.

"I'm Igor. A good friend of Fabian's. We go way back. I've started choreographing the routine Jen is going to perform. She'll need to make sure she concentrates solely on dancing. Any distraction could be detrimental." He smiles at her in an all-knowing way and it rattles me. Igor must have picked up on it because he continues, "I'm also the director of City of Lights Ballet Company. I hired Jen a few months back. She's very promising and I'm pleased she got this role."

LOVE IN B MINOR

"Were you involved from the beginning?" Jen asks, frowning like she's still trying to put all the pieces of the puzzle together.

"Fabian had asked me what I thought of choreographing a dance for a music video. He sent me the melody and I started working on it."

Jen squares her shoulder and plays with her hair, taking it down, putting it up again. "You could have told me. You probably already knew I got the part."

"Actually, I did not until you announced it to me this morning. I'm very pleased to be working with you on this. You've got the talent and the dedication and you can represent the School well...except I heard about this little drug incident of yours."

Jen doesn't gasp, she doesn't even flinch. She steels herself, her entire body tenses and I see how she protects herself, puts up a wall around her when she's attacked. She hasn't done that much around me until now.

Grégoire clears his throat—not because he's nervous but because he wants to make sure Igor knows who's in charge. "We haven't decided on the timeline to discuss this yet. We'll probably do a short written interview the day before the video releases," Grégoire says, his fists firmly planted in front of him on the table. It seems he wasn't aware this Igor guy was going to be involved as well.

Everybody sits down and we all get to work. Fabian explains his vision and how he'll have Jen dance to the song in different places. She'll be in front of the Eiffel Tower, and in a warehouse. In the light and in the darkness. Her dancing will be cut with Olivia and I singing by ourselves in the mountains. I need to call Mom and cancel Sunday lunch, since we're travelling to the Pyrenees.

Sadness and grieving will be the main message of the video, and then there will be some hope.

"Jen and I will work on the choreography every morning in the ballet studio of the company before the rehearsal for the show begins." Igor sounds like arguing with him would be a bad idea. "She can do it." But even though he's been an ass for a big part of this meeting, he does seem confident in Jen. I hope she sees that. That everyone believes in her.

LOVE IN B MINOR

Olivia stayed pretty silent the entire time and right before we all part ways, she slides next to me. "I'm going to go see Benji's grandmother at the hospital tomorrow morning, do you want to come with me?"

"I thought visits were only during the afternoon."

"I didn't want any craziness following me there, so I agreed with the hospital that I would go in the morning. I go every two days. Usually from ten to eleven."

Again, she surprises me. I go to see Benji's grandmother every week, usually after hours. Sometimes, she asks about him. Other times, she thinks he's outside playing soccer, or still in jail for stealing fancy clothes in a boutique close to them. But most of the times, she thinks he's outside, waiting to come in and visit. I never have the heart to tell her that he's not coming back. Ever.

"I think she'd be happy to see us both at the same time. She always asks about you when I go. But if you're busy, I understand."

"I don't know, Olivia. It's one thing to sing together for Benji, to do one last song, and another to go see his grandma together."

"You're right. I'm sorry I asked. It's…"

"What is it?"

"Sometimes it's so hard to be there and to see her. How she still hopes without hope and sometimes how she remembers everything."

"It is. I know what you mean. Maybe we could, one time," I tell her, but I'm still so unsure. Spending more time with Olivia isn't going to convince Jen I want nothing more from her. Even though it's true. When I look at Olivia I see my past. When I look at Jen, I see my present and I see my future.

"Sounds good." Olivia doesn't argue. She simply waves at me and leaves the room. I turn around and Jen's nowhere to be seen.

Shit.

I hurry out of the room and almost run into her. "I thought you left."

LOVE IN B MINOR

"You did tell me to wait for you. I just didn't want to impose and I understand you guys have things to talk about."

"Benji's grandmother has Alzheimer's, and both Olivia and I try to see her as often as possible. Sometimes, she doesn't remember anything, other times she remembers too much almost. It's hard. Olivia wanted to know if we could visit her together at some point."

I can't read her face. And it's killing me, because she's not letting me in, but then she exhales slowly. "I'm ready to go if you are." And she offers me a tiny smile.

I'll take what I can.

CHAPTER 36 – JEN

I'd like nothing more than to run and hide in my apartment. To fall into my bed and sleep everything off and wake up in the city, at the School of Performing Arts my very first semester. I'd redo everything, and then I'd find a way to save Mia.

But since that's not possible, since hiding is not a possibility, I put one foot in front of the other. At least I've learned and come to accept that you can't go back in time. The problem is I'm not sure Lucas is there yet. He hasn't grieved the death of his friend. Grieving is not about forgetting, but also about keeping that person close to you and moving on.

Somehow.

We walk outside of the building side by side but without a word. The same driver as the one who picked me up with him from the ballet company is waiting for us. Lucas opens the door for me and we slide into the car. The car still has that brand new leathery smell and the seats are cozy, but I can't relax. Lucas stares straight ahead. What is he thinking about?

"The song was beautiful." I break the silence— because even though I believe in silences that are comfortable, in not filling the silence with empty words, I also believe in reaching out. "It really was. And I think it's a beautiful tribute."

His shoulders relax and his hand finds mine. His hand is warm. His hands always seem to be warm while mine are always cold, and they fit perfectly together. They complete each other, like they've been looking for each other for a very long time.

And I need to stop making analogies between our hands and us.

"Thanks." His voice is low and careful. "I wrote that song three months after he passed away. The week after he died, Olivia and I went to Corsica."

"Grégoire mentioned one or two things about that." I'm dipping my toes into the murky water of their relationships.

He exhales loudly and his hand tenses in mine. "Did he tell you she lied about us getting engaged? How my parents got hounded like the bad guys when everyone wrote they were the reason we didn't get hitched. Even though it's far from the truth."

"No, someone overheard her saying that she wouldn't say no if you proposed and spread the gossip." My voice is barely above a whisper, because I'm not sure what his reaction is going to be.

"She used me before to gain more exposure. She even used Benji's death to advance her own solo career."

"That's not what Grégoire thinks happened. He thinks that was a cry for help, that she thought her starting fresh again would move you to continue singing." I pause, trying to choose my next sentences carefully because to be fair, I don't know what happened. "I can't tell you what the truth is. But after only one day in that world, it would not surprise me one bit if someone did overhear her and spread the story." I breathe the words out; they're fast but they're true.

He sighs and scoots closer to me—bridging the distance between us, at least physically. "I'm going to change the topic."

"Why?"

"Because we won't find the answers to those questions now. Because it's not necessarily fair of me to unload everything on you." I raise my hand to protest but he presses his lips to each of my knuckles softly, and it's like the entire air in the car has been shooed out. I'm feeling dizzy and I'm not sure if it's because I haven't eaten anything since this morning, or because of him. He leans back, keeping my hand in his. "What was your favorite cartoon when you were little? You told me that night that you loved cotton candy and that your favorite color is purple and that you would love to have a dog one day and one cat and that they would cuddle together and you would take the best pictures."

I squeeze his fingers and this time my smile isn't forced. "I would take the best pictures. I'd name my dog Baryshnikov and my cat Copeland."

"Those are long names."

"They're these amazing dancers that I wish I could emulate." I smile, imagining my cat and my dog. My dog would have those trusting eyes, and my cat would be fluffy. Both of them would be happy, and I'd take care of them. It's been a dream of mine to have pets for a long time, but my parents said we didn't have time.

"Favorite cartoon?"

"When I was about six years old, I was crazy about SpongeBob."

His eyes crinkle on the side. And his entire body seems more relaxed. And I've got to admit those questions are fun. It's funny how I have the feeling we've known each other for a long time, that we know each other so well. And maybe we do, on a deeper level—we already know what makes the other tick, we seem to recognize each other's expressions, but those questions? They remind me of that night. They show me a different side of him.

So I play along. "How about you?"

"I think it's a phase everyone goes through. Patrick was my favorite. Why did you start dancing?"

"Mom signed me up for a class when I was four. She said I loved it, that I was always jumping up and down before going to class like this was the best time of the week. Then, it became so much more. I was good at it. And I really loved it. And one day in my first year in middle school, I had a very bad day. Some guy was a total jerk to me and when I went to my ballet class, I was crying. My teacher took me to the side and told me to use my pain in my dancing. It became my one refuge." I turn to the side. Paris at night. The lights everywhere. "And then my first semester at the School of Performing Arts, when the kids there were mean to me, dancing wasn't enough anymore, because I wasn't enough for me. I had issues, lots of them and I didn't know how to deal with them." I glance down, lost in my thoughts, my voice almost cracking at the memories. "That's how I ended up looking for validation elsewhere. And…then the beach episode happened." I look back up, my voice firmer. "It took me a while, a lot of therapy hours to realize I needed to validate myself." I pause and touch his hand. "How about you? Why singing?"

"It all started with the piano. Mom played and she put me in early classes. Then, we made it a fun Wednesday evening ritual to play music together. She didn't push me but my teacher told me how good I was, and he encouraged me to come up with sounds depending on how I felt that day. I loved doing that, the music I was able to produce."

He shifts on his seat and his eyes find mine. I hold my breath for a second before releasing it. Once Emilia and I passed the awkward *We dated the same guy and you're still with him* phase, she told me Nick could see her, truly see her. I've never believed one look could unravel someone. But I am feeling pretty unraveled right now. His dark blue eyes are intense and they're focused on me and I need to get my thoughts together. "How old were you?" I'm surprised by how normal I manage to sound despite all the thoughts running through my mind.

"Eight." And finally he glances away, allowing my heart to return to a somewhat normal beating.

"You must have been the cutest eight-year-old on the piano."

He turns to me again, but I keep focusing on his hands. Which might not be the greatest idea either if I want to stay calm. He's got pianist hands, and hands that know exactly what they're doing. When they were slightly touching my skin, teasing me. How deliciously rough they could be. Time to stop staring at his hands. I look up and the corner of his mouth tilts up in a knowing smile "You could have danced to my tunes back then."

"I'm doing it now." And it's like we're having a totally different conversation in our heads that may have nothing to do with music and dancing, and when we both smile, my heart warms up. I'm aware of where its beat spreads. *Get a grip on your hormones, Jen.* "What's your favorite place in Paris?"

He puts one finger on his mouth, taps it twice before answering. "I have several. I can't choose. I love being around Notre Dame, because I can't imagine how people were able to build such a monument centuries ago, and because it has the spot where everything starts. I love the Luxembourg gardens when it's all quiet. And I have a new favorite spot."

"Where?"

"A bench by the Eiffel Tower where you begged me to bake cookies and where you told me that you were tired of pretending to play a role. When I asked you which role, you answered that not having answers was sometimes the best policy."

That night which was only three days ago almost seems like it was a lifetime ago. And the memories are like a fuzzy blanket you cover yourself with when you want to be cozy and warm and happy. "And then you kissed me."

"No, then *you* kissed me." His hand goes from my hand to my hair. "I love your hair. And I love how you always twist it up when you're trying to hide that you're stressed."

"I don't do that."

"Of course you do." He runs his fingers through my hair. Slowly, and if he doesn't stop I don't think I'll ever remember how to breathe correctly again. "I also love how your hair felt on me…"

I lick my lower lip. I need to change the topic, and fast. He's making it very hard to not jump on him. No pun intended. "Where are you taking me?"

"The other night, you said you haven't seen much of Paris. That you pretty much only work, work, work. And…"

"Sir, we've arrived." The driver clears his throat. "Actually, we've been here for about five minutes." There's laughter in his voice.

"Sorry, I was getting caught in the moment." And Lucas is also stifling a laugh; he doesn't look embarrassed or ashamed or anything but happy to be where he is. With me.

So, I'm just going to roll with it.

We step outside and I turn to him with flutters in my stomach. "Are we really doing this?"

"Definitely. I wanted to find a way to join the crowd, but then Steve said this might be too risky if someone recognize us, so I booked us a private cruise on the Seine. Dinner will be served—you said that your favorite meal was a lasagna from an Italian restaurant but that you also loved authentic Japanese food because it reminds you of your great-grandparents. Since I could not get that lasagna delivered on time, I got us a cook from one of my favorite Japanese places." He chuckles in an embarrassed manner, running his hand through his hair, shifting on his feet. I don't think he realizes how adorable he is, how thoughtful. "This is so sweet, thank you."

"Wait until you taste the oden he prepares, it's incredible."

"Very fitting for the weather. My favorite oden dish was the one my grandma made, she said it came from her region and on top of the boiled eggs, and the usual fishcakes and all that, but the broth is darker, she used broth that was flavored with beef stock and used dark soy sauce. She cooked it at least once a month for us during the winter." The cold air soaks through my sweatpants and I shiver.

"I got us blankets and hats in case we want to sit outside for a while. You'll see: Paris from the Seine at night is amazing."

He holds my hand in his as we go down the stairs and into a white boat.

An older lady with a chignon on top of her head welcomes us, wearing all white. "We're so happy to have you." And she does look happy. And maybe a bit starstruck too.

Lucas shakes her hand. "Thank you so much for agreeing to do this."

"We will be taking you on a two-hour tour, stopping by Notre Dame for about twenty minutes. We have a guide who will give you some history details and anecdotes about Paris as we glide through the Seine."

I turn to Lucas, pretty sure my excitement and amazement is reflected in his eyes. This is one of the best evenings ever. I've been meaning to see more of Paris. Every time I went with Mom, we only did some shopping and met with old friends of hers, but it was usually quick before heading to another city.

Lucas leads the way into the boat. A guy wearing black and a white apron appears out of nowhere—or maybe I was too focused on looking at everything to see him. "Would you like some champagne, maybe some kir?"

"A kir?"

"Champagne with your choice of liquor: raspberry, cassis…"

"Can I have one with raspberry, please?" I reply, and I'm hit by the beauty and history surrounding me. The stars in the sky are more visible than in the past days, and the wind blows but it's not as strong.

"Champagne for me, *s'il-vous-plaît*," Lucas answers and his arm sneaks around my waist. "What do you think?"

I lean into him. Thankful for this moment. Thankful for him. "This is amazing. Thank you so much."

LOVE IN B MINOR

"I've been wanting to do a river cruise for a while. The last time I went was with my grandparents when they came to visit years ago."

"The ones you told me about." While he was drunk in my apartment, he rambled about them. "You said you loved working on the ranch when you were younger."

"I did. It was hard, and definitely demanding but I loved spending time in the fields, taking care of everything. I still do it. Every single year for at least two weeks. I never talk about it."

"Why?" I accept the flute of kir the waiter brings us back, and Lucas gestures for us to sit outside. He grabs two blankets with one hand and we settle down at the end of the boat, with Paris surrounding us. This night is magical and could be surreal, but I am feeling everything. I'm living every second of this magical night. This has not happened in such a long time, for me to slow down and be there. I've tried so hard to live in the present, and it feels good that it's finally happening.

"I don't want to be reachable when I'm at their ranch." He raises his glass. *"A la tienne. A ta santé."* His lips curve into the smile I've already learned to seek. It's a happy smile, no restraints, and it's a smile so full of promises that my stomach fills with butterflies dancing to the music he created.

A voiceover explains the sights we're seeing. The Concord. The Louvre Museum. The voiceover says it could take up to one hundred days to see every piece of art that is in the Museum, if you spent thirty seconds at each piece all day, every day for those hundred days.

"Have you been there?" he asks, and his hand reaches out to my neck; it's a quick touch, a quick caress, but I'm suddenly no longer cold.

"Huh?" My question is more a sound than a word because he short-circuited my brain.

"At the Louvre?"

"With my mom. Last year, we went for a very quick visit to France because I was looking for companies. I didn't want to. I wanted to stay home. Mia was doing okay, but still. Every single day we spent away from home was hard. Mom felt so guilty."

LOVE IN B MINOR

"I felt guilty too…when Benji died. I thought…I thought I should have seen it coming. Because he was my best friend." I nod—waiting for him to say more, giving him the space to be silent if he needs to. He shakes his head from maybe unwanted thoughts. And we continue our travel through Paris.

I point to the bouquinistes by the Quai du Louvre. I've seen them only from afar, but I've been wanting to meander through the crowds looking at the books, enjoying the view, the Seine. Maybe eating at a small restaurant close by that serves crêpes bretonnes.

His fingers now trail down my arm—up and down—like a movement he's learned to love.

"Are you cold?" He gives me some of his blanket. Nope. You're definitely keeping me warm in all the right places. But I can't answer that.

"I'm fine." My stomach rumbles and I grimace when he laughs. "Oh come on, I haven't eaten since early this morning."

His eyes darken and cloud with worry. "You should have told me. I didn't realize you didn't have any lunch."

ELODIE NOWODAZKIJ

I bump my shoulder to his. "Did you bake me some cookies?" I bite my lip, not able to shake the picture of him—without a shirt, busying himself in his kitchen. That was one of the sexiest sights ever, not beating him entirely naked, though.

His chuckle is deep and full of unsaid words. "I wanted to, but I've been told to wait until we're done shooting that video."

Oh. "Are we still talking about cookies?"

There's a flash in his gaze that speaks volumes, and he stiffens against me as if he's trying to rein himself in. He inhales and exhales deeply. But before he answers, a voice speaks through the loudspeakers.

"You are currently under the Pont Neuf, which is the oldest bridge in Paris. You are basically under part of the history of Paris. The construction begun under Henri III in 1578, then halted in 1588 in the turmoil of the Wars of Religion. Henry IV continued its construction, as he believed in the importance of rebuilding Paris to end the division. Years later, it is said that Peter the Great declared he had found nothing more curious in Paris than the Pont Neuf while he came

to study French civilization under the regency of the
Duc d'Orleans. And for the Americans on this cruise,
you might be interested to know that the philosopher
Franklin wrote to his friends in America that he had not
understood the Parisian character except in crossing the
Pont Neuf."

I hold my breath to every word. "Can you
imagine all the stories that happened on this bridge?"

"My Dad told me once that …" He stops with a
smug smile. "And…wait, are you scared of
crocodiles?"

"Yes. I mean, no. We were in the Everglades
one year for the summer, after spending a weekend at
Disneyland. Mia was three years old and she ventured
out of the boat. I found her, sitting on the bench. Mom
and Dad could not hug us enough." This short holiday
was in between chemos for Mia, but back then she was
already a trooper and she smiled when she saw me. But
then we heard there had been a sighing of an alligator
close by. "Let's say I have a healthy fear of alligators."

"Dad read that in 1984, firemen working under the Pont Neuf bridge discovered something they never thought would live there."

"What was it?"

"A crocodile."

"What?" My mouth gapes open.

"It was a crocodile that was over one meter long, wandering about the sewerage system. Apparently, it was from the Nile and no one was ever able to explain how it got there."

"That's crazy. Wow. I'm going to be much more careful walking by the Seine now…" I smile. "You said both your parents love history. What do they do now?"

"Both Mom and Dad worked at Le Louvre. Mom writes historical fiction now. And Dad has become an expert on Greek art. He's in Greece right. I have come to love history thanks to them."

"My grandparents love to tell me about their stories. Some of them are sad, some are happy. I don't know it got me hooked on trying to learn more about the past."

LOVE IN B MINOR

The waiter reappears and I've forgotten about the wind, and the colder air. "We've arrived at Notre Dame. Your dinner is served inside."

I'm not quite sure how this evening could be topped.

But the promise of food is appetizing.

CHAPTER 37 - LUCAS

Seeing Paris through Jen's eyes is everything I'd hope for. She's interested, and amazed, and she doesn't try to look like she's seen it all already. She's...there. Not planning her next move. In the car, I had the hardest time—and that's an understatement—keeping from kissing her senseless. But after seeing the hurt in her eyes following my song performance with Olivia, I've realized her fear of getting hurt again. Being strong doesn't mean never being afraid. That's what Mom told me once when I was fourteen and scared shitless of playing on stage and then berating myself for not being strong enough.

Jen reminds me of that sentence. I don't want her to slip away. So, I'll play by her rules, and by Grégoire's rules. The video should be shot in less than two weeks depending on the choreography Igor has come up with.

Which makes me think. "Do you think Igor is going to let you choreograph with him?"

She startles, her fork in midair. "What do you mean?"

"The dance you came up with was amazing, and you had never even heard the melody."

"Some of the movements were out of synch," she protests, but there's a light in her eyes like she's intrigued.

"But you got the feelings...the most important part of the dance."

"Thank you." Her smile graces her entire face and simply looking at her inspires me to write another song. A song about finding solace, finding happiness, finding the person who walks by your side. Equals.

Lovers. Friends. "Honestly, I'm not sure if he will. I think he might ask for my opinion, but he'll only take what works. Even though he's a complete ass, I trust his artistic eye." She tilts her head to the side in her I'm-analyzing-you movement. "What were you thinking about like ten seconds ago? You were staring at me, but I didn't think you were there or seeing me."

"Oh no, I was seeing you. I thought of another song."

Her lips turn into a shit-eating grin. "The one-night-stand-who-gets-away-but-ends-up-at-your-audition?"

"You think that's funny." Laughter rumbles through me.

"A little. We both gave each other fake names. Clearly, you didn't think we'd see each other again." She eats the appetizer that was already on the table and closes her eyes. "This is delicious."

I could watch her for hours. I could talk to her for hours. I could discover her body for hours. My voice is much rougher than expected when I manage to speak again. "I wanted to see you. I had planned on telling you everything in the morning, so when I realized you left, I was disappointed. The song I'm thinking about writing now would be entitled, 'You.'"

She licks her lips. "I know we said we wouldn't be talking about sad stories, or anything. But I've got to ask." She licks her lower lip again and then slightly bites it. "Are you really okay? With what I told you? There are moments where I think that you look at me and you're unsure…I don't know, maybe of my motivations. Like you're afraid I'm here for another reason than…" She shakes her head, staring at her glass. "It's stupid."

I want to tell her it's not stupid. I want to tell her how hard it is for me to trust anyone.

My phone rings but I ignore it. Jen's eyes find mine again and she opens her mouth. She's about to say what she has in her mind or in her heart, or surprise me again with an unexpected comment.

"Sir," the waiter who has been so discreet until now comes in the restaurant. "Sir, there's a phone call from you. It's from Olivia McRae. She said it's important."

"Can't you take the message?"

"I'm sorry, sir. She said you'd want to talk to her—it's about Benjamin's grandmother."

My blood freezes and I brace myself for the worst. Jen pulls her chair close to me, and if it was anyone else, I might have pushed her away, but when she puts her hand on my thigh, I relish her presence. "Olivia? What's going on?"

"The hospital called me, they said they couldn't reach you." She doesn't sound accusatory but I still feel like I need to explain why. She doesn't give me any time to do so. "Steve gave me the number of the boat— you need to come back. Soon. Grand-mère Julie is not doing well. She fell from her bed, and apparently that brought on a heart attack and she's in a coma now. They don't know if she's going to make it." Her voice breaks. "I don't want to lose her."

My heart hurts and it takes all I have to not throw the phone away and scream. "I know. I'm coming back."

"Okay. Thank you."

LOVE IN B MINOR

"No, thank you. For calling me." And I hang up, lowering my head on Jen's knees. She wraps her arms around me, not asking any questions. Waiting, running her fingers on my back. She calms me down. I look up, not hiding how fucking sad I feel. Sad and raw. "It's Benji's grandmother."

"Oh, no. Let me tell the captain to get back to the dock. Why don't you call the driver to make sure he's waiting for you?"

"For us?"

"What?" She stumbles.

"Would you come with me to the hospital? Please?" I need her. I don't care about any of the rules we've set up for ourselves. I need her. With me.

And I don't care if it scares me shitless.

CHAPTER 38 - JEN

Lucas spends the drive to the hospital on the phone with Olivia. He looks worried, and exhausted, and devastated.

He rushes inside and I follow him. Olivia's waiting for him in the lobby and she throws herself into his arms. They hold each other, crying. And my heart aches for them. For both of them. Olivia's tears are real. Her sniffles and broken voice are real. Her pain is real.

When she sees me, she offers a soft smile. But we don't speak. Lucas turns back to me and hugs me tightly, telling me he needs to speak with the doctors.

LOVE IN B MINOR

"Do you want me to go with you?"

He simply takes my hand in his and I follow. The hospital smells, the nurses and doctors, everything reminds me of Mia. Of her time at the hospital. Of how she spent more time there than at home. And I'm the one gripping his hand now. I want to comfort him. I do, but it's hard for me to be there. To be invaded with images of Mia in her hospital bed, attached to tubes, still fighting to keep a smile on her face, because she didn't want us to be sad.

The entire conversation with the doctors takes place in French and I don't understand any of it. Lucas does translate a few words here and there and even Olivia does too, like she actually cares if I'm feeling left out or not. But right now, I don't. I'm here for Lucas.

After a few minutes, we go back to the lobby. "She's getting operated on now." Lucas' tone is like the beginning of the melody of his song about Benji. It's the saddest tone I've heard from him. "She used to make French toast for us. Not the one with the sliced bread, but she would take old stale bread and bake it in the oven. It was so good."

Olivia plops herself on a chair, brings her legs close to her and hugs them tight. "She always told us we had to work hard, but that we had to remember to also have fun. She always said you can fall in love when you're young, but that it shouldn't prevent you from living life." I'm not sure if she's talking to us or to herself.

Lucas continues as if they're finishing each other's thoughts. "She met her husband when she was thirteen. Love at first sight and they were married for fifty years before he died in an accident." Lucas leans into me and I wrap my arms around him. "She was always a rock for Benji, a rock for all of us. If she doesn't make it…"

I can't reassure him completely. I can't tell him she's going to recover because I don't know. But I can tell him what I believe, how he's helping her even if he doesn't realize it. "She knows you're here. I'm sure she knows."

LOVE IN B MINOR

"Why don't you go home? You've got a rehearsal early in the morning, I'm going to stay here and wait."

"I can wait." My lips touch his temple. "I can stay."

"Thank you," he whispers and he closes his eyes.

Olivia clears her throat. "Steve told me you lost a sister." Her voice is soft. Like she understands my pain.

I nod. "I did. Less than a year ago."

Olivia stares at her hands. "I don't know if you've read about me or if Lucas told you."

Lucas stiffens next to me "I didn't talk about it."

"And I promised myself to stay away from gossip magazines," I reply with a smile. Everyone has something they don't like to talk about, something buried deep inside.

"I had a little brother."

"Olivia," Lucas whispers and opens his eyes. They're full of sadness. Sadness for her.

"I just want to say I understand how hard it must be for you." A tear falls down her cheek and she wipes it away, straightening herself as if she's trying to stay strong. "I lost my little brother when he was about two years old. They don't know why. A doctor said my mom might have been negligent, might have shaken him too hard. He was crying a lot and our nanny was not there that night…and…I was sixteen. It was hard."

"I'm so sorry," I tell her and I mean every word. And now when I look at her, I see so much more than Lucas' ex—she's hurting too, and for many reasons.

"Me too. I didn't mean to come between you two. I didn't know…at the audition. I didn't know it was serious." And then she leans back in her chair. Lucas squeezes my hand.

We spend the rest of the night waiting—until the doctor comes back with good news. "She's awake and she wants to see you both," he says. "But only for a few seconds."

Lucas stands up, unsteady on his legs at first and then hugs me, whispering in my ear. "Thank you for staying." He glances behind me. "It's already six in the morning—let me call the driver for you. You need to go home, what time is your rehearsal?"

"Nine." And a yawn escapes me. Lucas dozed on and off but I couldn't close my eyes.

"Go, you should go. I'm okay. I promise." He slightly touches the top of my head with his lips and gives me another hug. "I'll tell the driver to be there as fast as possible. I'll call you later, okay?"

I wince remembering I still don't have a new number. "Can you call Alisha's phone? Or the company? I'll be there all day. Fabian said shooting for me won't start until next week."

"We start today." He rubs the back of his neck and I rise on my tippy toes, planting a soft kiss on his cheek.

"I'm there for you. You can also pass by if you want. I'll be back home around five today." I pause. "Or I could come back here."

"I'll call you." He squeezes my hand again as if he doesn't want to let me go but then slightly nudges me to the side. "Let me call the driver."

CHAPTER 39 - LUCAS

Seeing Jen leave is hard. It's funny and weird how in such a short time, she became a calming factor for me. It's like with her I don't have to worry about being who I am, showing her who I am.

"Monsieur Wills?" The doctor in charge of Benji's grandmother's care calls my name. Both Olivia and I stand up.

"Vous pouvez me suivre," he says we can follow him, so we do. Olivia clutches her side as if she's trying not to break down and I know the feeling.

LOVE IN B MINOR

I wish I could reassure her, tell her everything is going to be okay, but I can't. She sniffles but doesn't say anything. Grand-mère Julie was so important, is so important for us, and not only because she's our last link with Benji.

"*Cinq minutes.*" The doctor opens the door and my chest squeezes so tight I don't think I'll ever be able to breathe normally again. Grand-mère Julie looks so frail, so small, so helpless. She used to stand up to Benji, to keep him in check, to not only coddle him but also to try to give him a sense of direction, of purpose.

Her eyes flutter open. "Lucas, Olivia." I have to lean in to hear her. I touch her hand and Olivia's hand carefully falls on her shoulder.

"*Les amoureux,*" she whispers. "*Les amoureux...*" The lovers, that's what she used to call us when we were sixteen and stealing kisses in her kitchen.

"Benjamin." Her voice cracks. "*Mort.*" She remembers Benji is dead and that shatters my heart.

"*Ça va aller, Grand-mère Julie. Ça va aller.*" Olivia caresses her forehead, and then she glances at me with the saddest smile. Her mouth opens and she sings one of the first songs I ever wrote. It was a song about falling in love. At the time, I thought she and I would be together forever.

Grand-mère Julie closes her eyes and smiles, so I join Olivia in singing.

Hoping that Grand-mère Julie pulls through.

CHAPTER 40 - JEN

I've never noticed how many cracks there are on the ceiling of the ballet company's rehearsal room until now. Maybe because I've never raised my eyes to the ceiling as many times before.

Igor is tough and demanding. And my entire body aches. And he can't stop yelling.

"That pirouette was pitiful. Pitiful. You're supposed to extend your arms at the end—show the hurt that you're feeling, the devastation at losing someone." He stomps his foot to the ground like a toddler in crisis. I'd smile if he wasn't right. My pirouette was pitiful, but it's hard to concentrate when you're so tired and when the music reminds you of so much tragedy. "I really thought you would be the best for this role, that you would get how important it is to show the pain, the difficulty of moving on."

"I get it." My voice remains calm and I'm tempted to undo my hair, to put it up again. Something, anything to keep me busy.

"If you get it, why am I not transported? Why do I see the technique but not the emotion?" He gestures with his hands widely in the air. Audrey pokes her head inside the room, clears her throat.

"The rehearsal for the show starts in thirty minutes."

"Then, we have twenty minutes. I assume you brought a sandwich that you can eat in ten minutes."

"I didn't." Because I didn't realize I would only have a ten-minute break between one rehearsal to the other.

"Audrey, can you please get her one at the bakery next door?" His tone is more subdued when he speaks to her, but then turns harsher again when he turns to me. "You need your sleep. You need your rest. You've got to realize not only your career is on the line, but this company too."

My chin juts down automatically because he's right. I know he's right. But it's not like I could leave Lucas in the hospital, when he asked me to be with him.

Audrey steps in the room. "What sandwich would you like, Jen?"

"The ham and cheese one, please. I'll reimburse you before leaving. Thank you so much." I've been learning the new choreography for the past four hours now. And part of me stayed with Lucas. "Has anyone called for me?" I don't look at Igor when I ask, not wanting to see his reaction. I'm pretty sure using the company's phone for my own personal use would be frowned upon.

Audrey shakes her head. "No phone calls for you personally." She tilts her head to the side. "But there have been some calls from journalists—asking if we had any comments about you joining the music video and about someone being at the hospital?"

"What?"

"Apparently, there are pictures of Lucas Wills and you at the hospital, holding on to one another." She clears her throat again. "In one of them, it looks like you're looking straight at the camera."

Shit. Shit, shit, shit.

I didn't even think there could be journalists or photographers or people taking pictures in such a tragic moment.

If Lucas has seen those, he's going to be devastated. Having his privacy invaded while he's in despair, especially after everything that's happened. I don't get it.

I hang my head low, not sure what to say, or what to do. I don't even have my phone with me since I promised Mom this morning per email I wouldn't be reading any more messages. Apparently, they get worse as it goes.

Igor curses under his breath in a mix of Russian and French—I only recognize *Fuck.* "I'm going to say this only once, Jennifer." His tone is much calmer than during our entire rehearsal, but sometimes a calmer tone coming from him is scarier. "You better not have anything to do with this. I know I said the company needed to gain more exposure, but this is not the way to do it."

His words don't register.

"Jennifer, I'm serious." And he sounds serious.

Surprise leaves me speechless for a second, but then anger and incomprehension simmers beneath the surface and my voice turns icier than the wind we've had in Paris. "I would never ever do this." I glare at him. "Never."

Igor stares back at me as if trying to see deep within me if I'm lying or not, and then his shoulders slacken. "Fine. I believe you, but first your name is leaked to bloggers before Grégoire announces it, and then these pictures. I don't think Lucas will take kindly to being used."

"I'm not using him. I have no reasons to use him!" I clutch my sides, realizing that Lucas might not believe me. I hope he will. But with everything that's happened to him before, and with his deep mistrust of people, why would he trust me?

"Fine." Igor raises his hand in a calming way. "I told you I believe you. Just be careful out there. That world isn't all shiny and happy people. Jealousies run high." And he seems like he speaks from experience. He breathes out and steps forward. This time his eyes are kinder. "Listen, make sure you prepare yourself. There will be waves, there will be criticisms, people trying to destroy you because they want what you have."

I force a smile on my face. "It sounds like you're talking about ballet."

"You have a point." He squares his shoulders back and I know this little moment is over. "I have Grégoire's number—you can call him."

Like that's going to help me. Before I can reply, he claps his hands twice.

"Enough talking. Do half of the routine one more time, and I want you to lose yourself in the movements, use the anger you feel to channel it toward dancing. Let go."

And I do.

LOVE IN B MINOR

And even though I manage to dance the routine much better than before, there's still a nasty little voice in my head that tells me nothing is going to be as easy as it seems.

That it's only the beginning.

CHAPTER 41 – LUCAS

I slam my fist on the table, staring at the picture of Jen and I cuddled up on the chairs of the hospital. "This is fucking ridiculous. They can't do that!"

Olivia and I stayed at the hospital until midafternoon, waiting to see Grand-mère Julie again. We've been civil to one another, and having Olivia there was important. Important for Grand-mère Julie, who is lost in a time that is long gone. In a time where Olivia and I were ready to take on the world with Benji by our side. She asked for him once and then chuckled, saying she should remember he was rehearsing.

LOVE IN B MINOR

As soon as we left the hospital, we got caught in a social media frenzy. Someone posted that picture on Snapchat and it turned viral. They're playing up the fact that Jen's the one who's been chosen for that video. And right now I wish, I really wish we could postpone it, but everything is already set in motion.

Olivia stands in the corner of the room. "We need to let Jen know that it's happened." Her voice is soft but her eyes are shooting daggers. "Trust me, I'm well placed to know how hard being in the spotlight can be."

Steve rolls his eyes and mutters under his breath, still loud enough that everyone in the room can hear him. "You also learned how to use the spotlight." Thought he wasn't in the band when all the shit went down, I told Steve how difficult the months following Benji's death have been, how breaking up with Olivia may have been the right thing to do but how hard it was for me to come to the realization that she wasn't the one.

Olivia flinches at his words and glances down. "What I'm saying is that sometimes having your name printed across the paper like this isn't easy to deal with."

Grégoire plops back down on a chair and holds his iPad up to look at the picture again. "She does look like she's staring straight into the camera. How could she have not seen it?"

"People take pictures with everything these days. IPad, iPod, phones…she may not have realized this was someone invading her privacy." Olivia steps forward and sits at the table too.

"I should call her." I rub the back of my neck. I've been so preoccupied with Grand-mère Julie and with that new picture that I haven't tried to call her yet.

"How about you wait until after your meeting with Fabian. You said she was rehearsing anyways. She may not even know about it yet." Grégoire swipes in his iPad. "We need to find a narrative for the story about her using drugs in the past." And then he taps his fingers on the table. "Is there anything else I should know?"

Olivia winces. But doesn't say a word.

"Olivia?" Grégoire stares at her.

LOVE IN B MINOR

"I got a weird email this morning. I only read it ten minutes ago and I didn't want to bring it up right now but…"

"What?"

"Someone says they have pictures of Benji…" She gulps as if the next words are hard for her to say. "Pictures of Benji dying."

The air around me is gone. I don't think I can breathe correctly. "What the fuck? What do they want? Why send them to you?"

"I don't know. And I don't have them. All that email says is that we should be careful who to trust." Her body shakes and her fingers tremble when she shows us the email. Her voice is full of tears. "I don't know who would do that. I know people hate me, hate us, but to go that far?"

I slam my fist against the table again. "This is so much bullshit."

"We knew that a comeback was going to be difficult. We knew it and we accepted it." Grégoire sounds reasonable. "Why don't you guys go meet with Fabian, he wants to take a few shots today, and plan the trip to the Pyrenees for the mountain shots, and I'll try to get to the bottom of this." His eyes dart from me to Olivia. "I'll let you know in case anything changes with Miss Julie. And don't worry, I'll handle this."

That's when I'm grateful Grégoire is in our corner. Because no matter how many stories he plants himself, he's also a pro at dealing with the bullshit that comes along.

Steve walks by me on our way to our meeting. "Are you sure you're okay, bro?"

"I'll be fine. For some odd reason, it makes me want to sing that song even more." I shake my head. "It doesn't make sense, but it makes me feel like it's the right thing to do for Benji. For him to know somehow that we're still in this together, that I won't let him down and let his legacy be tarnished by his last moments."

"I get it." Steve pats my shoulder. "Just make sure you don't hurt yourself in the process."

Easier said than done.

CHAPTER 42 - JEN

I'm exhausted by the time the rehearsals for the final show are done. My legs shake as I walk, and I yawn every few minutes.

"How is the lady doing?" Alisha asks. She let me use her phone as soon as she got there, but I left a voice mail. I still didn't hear anything from Lucas, and there's a sinking in my stomach that there's something wrong.

"When I left, she was awake but I haven't gotten any news."

"Steve told me they were working on the song about Benji together with Olivia and then looking at a few shots this afternoon. He texted me before their meeting with Fabian." She has a dreamy look on her face and I squeeze her hand.

"You sound happy."

"Nope, I sound like I'm willing to take a chance. Steve's been…nice and understanding. I saw him yesterday for dinner."

"Oh…"

She swats my arm playfully and her cheeks flush slightly. "Well, we didn't go on a dinner cruise on the Seine, but it was nice. Really nice."

"Nice is good." I link my arm with hers and instead of stepping into the courtyard, we take the back exit. There are still a few people set on asking me questions about last night, about whatever is going on, and I don't feel like putting on a show.

I managed to call the therapist's office during the ten minutes Igor gave me for lunch and I got an appointment for tomorrow. I know myself well enough to realize that once all this adrenaline and this robotic-keep-going mode slows down, I might crash. And I can't crash. I don't want to crash.

Snow flurries are falling down and I tilt my head back. "I always loved snow."

"It is nice until it becomes all muddy." Alisha wrinkles her nose when she says "muddy." She comes from California and is always craving a seventy degrees climate and sunny and the waves of the ocean.

"How are you really doing?"

I haven't told her yet about what the press might reveal soon, and I don't want to talk about it outside, so instead I tell a half-truth. "Exhausted. Physically and mentally drained."

Her cell phone rings and she smiles—it's not a big smile, it's one of those smiles that says she's trying to keep her happiness close to her because she's afraid it's going to pop and disappear. I get it.

"It's Steve. Lucas wants to talk to you."

My heart jumps carefully. I'm not sure how he's going to react about our picture taken together. "Hey…"

"Hi Laura slash Jen." His voice is sad but warm and my heart jumps higher. "How did the rehearsals go?"

"Good. I mean Igor thought that I sucked, but overall I think good."

He clears his throat at the same time I clear mine. "Go ahead," he says.

"I saw the pictures. I'm so sorry about what you must have gone through today. How is Grand-mère Julie doing?"

"She's doing better. Much better, actually."

"I'm so glad to hear that."

"As for the pictures, I should have known someone might have been there. I always have to be on my guard."

"I'm sorry I didn't see anything."

"I know you are. I'd love to see you tonight, but I'm going to go back to the hospital."

"I could come with you."

"I think it's best I go alone." He breathes out. "I wish you could be there, but between what happened with the pictures, and your schedule, I don't want to ask again."

"Yesterday, you didn't ask." My voice is soft like the beginning of the song he wrote about our night. "I offered. Today, I am offering too. You shouldn't have to do this alone."

He hesitates for a second. "Olivia will be there," he replies and there's a pinch in my heart. "I'd love to see you before I leave though."

"How about you pass by before going to the hospital tonight?"

"I wish I could, but we have to go back to the studio. We only have a two-minute break."

"I'll call you or text you. Grégoire got you a new phone with a new number, it should be delivered to your apartment tonight."

"Thank him for me."

"I will." His voice turns lower, like he doesn't want anyone to hear it. "I'm going to miss you. Is that crazy?"

"I don't think so. I hope not. Because I'm going to miss you too."

Alisha makes kissing sounds next to me and I chuckle.

"Bye, Jennifer Harrison. Wait, what's your middle name? Tell me it's Laura."

I don't want to hang up, so I stop walking. "My middle name is Sana—like my great-grandmother."

"So why Laura?"

"It's a stupid story."

"Oh come on…" There's a smile in his voice and hearing him happier warms my entire body.

"About two years ago, I was having coffee in the city. I was by myself and some random dude hit on me…and his first line was 'Please tell me your name is Laura because my psychic told me I was going to meet a Laura today.' When I told him my name wasn't Laura, he then said, 'Then you must be the angel she said I would kiss.'"

Lucas cracks up and I do too…that guy didn't understand why I didn't give him my number.

"That makes sense. And that's a much better story than me using my middle name."

LOVE IN B MINOR

There's a scuffle in the background and the very annoyed voice of Grégoire comes through. Something about Lucas needing to remember his priorities.

"Go," I whisper. "I'll hang up."

"Okay. I'll talk to you later tonight or tomorrow."

"Bye." And I hang up quickly because if had waited, I think I'd fall asleep with the phone in my hand.

I ignore the alarm in my head reminding me how much Olivia and he have in common. I ignore the alarm in my heart telling me I could get hurt again. And I ignore the alarm screaming in stereo in my ears that I need to remember that falling for Lucas could be a bad idea.

Because what if it isn't?

What if taking a risk is what I need?

I'm already falling.

CHAPTER 43 – LUCAS

The studio is even fancier than the last one we used. The leather couches are comfy, the table in front of us has a basket full of fruits and fresh pastries. And there's this brand new smell. The studio was renovated recently. The walls are covered with awards and with pictures of famous French singers with the producers.

Olivia's running slightly late and she rushes inside the room. Everyone—Steve, Dimitri, Grégoire and Fabian—turns to look at her. "Sorry. Sorry I'm late. Lucas, can I talk to you quickly?"

LOVE IN B MINOR

Grégoire pushes the guys inside the studio—except Fabian, who stands with his crew and the music producer behind the glass.

There are tears in Olivia's eyes, and I've seen her cry only a handful of times before. When we were looking for Benji and when he was found dead, when she told me about her little brother dying and when her pictures got stolen from her cell phone. When we broke up, she tried very hard to not show me her tears. She ran off. "What's wrong?"

Olivia tugs my shirt. "Whoever sent the pictures of Benji released them. They're online. Don't look. Don't look at them." She sniffles and I pull her into a hug. She sobs in my arms and for a split second, I'm back in those terrible days. Days that never seemed to end.

"I'm sorry you saw them. I'm sorry you saw them," I repeat and I caress her hair in a comforting way. "Let's tell Grégoire so he knows and then"—I tilt her chin up and try to use a soothing and calming voice—"and then we concentrate on the music. Because that's what Benji would have wanted, okay?"

She nods and I pull her inside with me. After we tell Grégoire, we both keep our word and focus on the music.

Being in the studio is like living in a bubble. For hours, I forget the time, I forget everything. I let myself get wrapped up in the music, lose myself in the music.

"This is fucking awesome," Steve yells and then throws his fist up the air. "We're absolutely killing it." And then he stops and his eyes dart to me. "What I meant to say is…"

I cut him off, because right now, he's right.

Everything makes sense again. The music, the band. My eyes dart to Olivia. And her smile is small, but it's there.

"It's an amazing song," she says and her laugh is forced at first but then turns into her signature giggle. "Much better than the first one we ever wrote together, do you remember?"

"You mean, the one that rhymed everything with blue?"

"Tell me it wasn't a masterpiece."

LOVE IN B MINOR

And I laugh along with her. Because we do need to move on. Somehow.

CHAPTER 44 – JEN

My new cell phone is delivered early evening and after catching up with my parents and Emilia, I text Lucas and wait for his call. I re-watch old episodes of *Parks & Rec*, chuckling every few minutes. But soon enough my eyes can't stay open. And I crash. My dreams are a mix of the past and the future. Mia smiles as she meets Lucas, but then Lucas runs off, telling me we will never work. He runs into Olivia's arms.

And there's a loud buzz. I swat the bee that's trying to sting me but it keeps on darting back. I turn around and fumble to find my phone. Morning came way too fast. But it's not my phone either. And it's only nine in the evening.

I grab a sweater and tiptoe outside of bed, relishing the hardwood floor under my feet because it means I was indeed dreaming.

I press the intercom. "Who is this?"

"It's me." Lucas' voice does things to my insides, but then worry takes over.

"Is everything okay? Is Grand-mère Julie okay?"

"She is. She's great actually. We got some shitty news about pictures of Benji being leaked but that's not why I'm here. I just wanted to see you before leaving tomorrow."

"Come on up." I buzz him in and there's no nervousness in my chest, just a happy feeling I could get used to. Quickly.

A few seconds later, I let him my apartment. It's weird how he already looks like he belongs, like it's perfectly normal for him to come over. Maybe because I feel like we're friends…even with this intense chemistry between us, we're friends.

I wrap my arms around him and he hugs me back tightly. His breath tickles my neck and I cuddle closer. His body against mine is strong and I melt against him. I entirely melt against him: my body, my mind, my heart.

He steps back first and softly kisses my lips.

My mouth forms an "o." "I thought we needed to obey the rules."

"Screw the rules. Shit, life is too short."

"I usually obey the rules…" I blabber. The only time I didn't follow them, I almost died of an overdose. But then he kisses me again and I forget everything.

His energy is all over the place, like I'm helping him forget the pain. His hands are in my hair, his mouth is on my neck. His lips trail down my shoulder and I moan loudly.

I pull him with me and we end up on the couch. His fingers trace an imaginary design on my stomach while mine struggle with his jeans. Instead, I pull on his shirt and he takes it off. My hands explore every inch of him. I never want to stop.

LOVE IN B MINOR

"Shit, my fucking phone." His lips touch mine again softly. I'm breathing hard and so is he. "It could be the hospital, I have to get it." He shakes his head, annoyed. "Stupid Grégoire." His phone beeps with a text and then rings again.

Lucas rubs the back of his head in his signature I'm annoyed move. "What do you want?"

He listens intently. "You're fucking kidding me. Of course, it's not her." He nods and glances my way. "Uh-huh. How is Olivia doing? Okay, uh-huh."

And then he hangs up. He stays on his phone for a few more seconds, his face blanching.

"Can I ask you something?"

Okay. This is not how I expected the evening to continue. "Of course. What's going on?"

"So if we did wait to get together, when would we be able to?"

"What?" I raise both eyebrows as high as I kick my leg in an arabesque

"I'm gone for the week, then we film the rest of the video within three days and then we're done, right?"

"There's that show at my ballet company." And then I want to take the words back, because he stares at me in such a way that I feel like he's questioning everything, like he's questioning me.

"What if I didn't do it?"

"Why?" I'm tempted to say it's okay, that I understand, but I don't. Before I might have let it go, I might have smiled and pretended I'm fine. That's what I would have done with Nick, but I feel more myself around Lucas than anyone else, and I don't want to lose that because I'm afraid to lose him. "Why wouldn't you do it?"

"Is that what you want?" he asks and his voice is bitter and I don't understand it.

And this throws me off. I thought we were getting closer. "I don't know—you tell me." My tone is harsh but that's either that or I let my voice break. "You have to explain because I'm lost."

"Here." He hands me his phone.

And I read the headline of the new trashy website that gathers millions of views every single day.

LOVE IN B MINOR

Olivia McRae's brother died because of their mother's negligence.

"What?" My eyes widen and I'm still lost. It's not the first time and it won't be the last something shitty is written about him, about them.

"The only people who know some of the details inside that article are you, Olivia, Benji and me. And Benji is dead, so you do the math."

"I didn't say anything to anyone." I flinch. His words sting more than the bee from my nightmare. "I wouldn't blabber. It must have been Olivia. She's done it before, right?"

"She would never say anything about her brother, just like I hope you would never say anything to the press about your sister."

That's a slap in the face. "Don't tell me what I can and cannot say about Mia. Don't you dare bring Mia into this."

He rubs the back of his head and walks to the other side of the room; he's pacing. "I don't want to believe you had any hand in that article."

"Then don't believe it, because I didn't. Can you tell me why would I do that? I don't want to hurt you and I don't even understand the appeal of being in those magazines. Maybe it's Grégoire."

"Maybe it's all about that show, your company." His voice is sad and unsure and I want to shake him, because what the heck? I wrap my hair up in a knot, not caring he knows that's what I do when I'm stressed. How did he go from almost making love to me to being mad at me? For something I didn't even do.

I stand up, step toward him. "This show could save the company. It could save the jobs of my friends. Of course I want you to do this show. I don't understand why you're so pissed." Anger now rises within me. I clench my fists before showing him the door. "Honestly, I don't know what you're thinking, but the simple fact you think I could do that is beyond me."

He shifts on his feet. "It's not just that. Grégoire said Igor was not the one who leaked the news about you getting the role."

LOVE IN B MINOR

"And you think I did that too? You think I want my private life on display?" I seethe. "I would tell you I don't care about the show, but it would be a lie. It's not only me who's on the line with you joining our last dance. It's the entire company." I throw my arms in the air when he still doesn't answer and point to the door. "You have to go. You have to think about everything you just told me, and then you have to think if you've really moved on."

"Moved on?"

"Even if you're over Olivia—which I'm still not sure you are. You're clearly not over the fact she used you. I'm not Olivia the Second. I won't be Olivia the Second." I take a deep breath. "Now, get out. I'll see you next week for the filming by the Eiffel Tower."

He opens his mouth but I don't want to hear it.

I close the door behind him. I don't slam it because my anger is already receding into hurt. I lean against the door and let the tears fall.

CHAPTER 45 – LUCAS

I'm tempted to knock at Jen's door and ask her to forgive me for doubting her, but the thing is: my doubts linger. Olivia would never speak about her brother that way. She told me about a year after we started dating, and she was crying so hard. The pain was still raw; it's not a story you go blabber about. And Grégoire wouldn't want to rehash that particular past, and then there's another small article talking about my love for *Parks & Rec.* It's too much coincidence. I only started watching it after breaking up with Olivia, so she doesn't know about it. But the look on Jen's face? That look was a mix of anger, hurt and confusion.

I march back to my apartment. Not closer to any solution.

Maybe it's a sign we need to take it more slowly, maybe it's a sign I jumped into this too fast. So what if she's the only who's made me feel alive in months?

In front of my door, there's a silhouette sitting with her head in her arms. "Olivia?" I ask and the form moves. Her tears break my heart. No matter the time that has passed and the hurt between us, seeing her sad still pulls at my heartstrings.

"What's wrong? Is it Grand-mère Julie?"

"No, it's about that article…Mom saw it and she went into her depression mode thinking about Cody." She sniffles and I take her hand in mine, pulling her up with me.

"Come on, let me make you some hot chocolate with marshmallows." And there's a hint of a smile on her face. It was always her favorite.

"Can you add some whiskey?"

"Sure thing, I think I need it today."

And we hobble upstairs. We're both exhausted after spending so much time at the hospital and rehearsing and Olivia simply wants to talk about her brother. So, I let her talk and when her eyes start to close, she asks if she can stay over. Sending her away while she's so sad doesn't seem right—especially when she explains how alone she feels right now—so I let her sleep on my bed, while I take the couch.

Until the next morning, when my doorbell rings. Olivia's up before me. She's making her signature crêpes. "Do you want me to get it?"

"That'd be great." I turn and crack my neck. The couch really isn't that comfortable.

She hurries to the door. "Bonjour."

"Lucas?" I recognize Jen's voice. "Olivia?" And then before I can get to the door and tell her that nothing's happened, "I get it. I'll see you guys next week, have fun during your trip."

I would go after her, but I'm still way too unsure about the leaks. It's now the third one, and every single time she's involved. It can't be a coincidence.

LOVE IN B MINOR

Olivia frowns and she glances up at me, with one side of her mouth tilted to the right in her *I'm sorry* way. "Do you want me to talk to her? I can if you want."

"No, that's fine. I'm unsure about everything right now anyways."

"Why? Talk to me. Last night you only said you were worried you were getting too close too fast." She pauses and her hand reaches out...it's like an automatism, she used to caress my cheek with two fingers whenever she wanted me to pay attention. Her hand drops before touching me and she glances away. "Are you worried she might hurt you like I did?" She clears her throat, still not looking at me. "I've done a lot of wrong. To you, to a lot of people."

And then because I need to know, I ask. "All those rumors about you and Benji?"

This time her eyes find mine and her shoulders square back. "They weren't true. Of course they weren't true."

And I want to believe her. I want to believe my best friend and my girlfriend didn't go at it behind my back. I want to believe they didn't betray me.

I've had enough betrayals for a lifetime.

CHAPTER 46 - JEN.

When my doorbell rings, I think it's Lucas coming back to apologize, but it's Olivia. Her eyes are red and she's not wearing any makeup.

I open the door, poking my head out. "What do you want?" My tone could be more welcoming, but it has been a hard day.

She glances down and then back at me. "I just want to let you know that nothing happened between Lucas and me." She tilts her head. "Can I come in? I'll be quick I promise."

I let her inside my apartment. She's got circles under her eyes. And she shifts from one foot to another, she's far from the confident Olivia I've seen before. I'm not sure which one is the real one or if like the rest of us, she's made of many layers and is still learning who she is. "Your apartment looks nice." She glances around and then winces as if she's not happy with what she said. "Okay, the walls are kind of bare and it's a bit sad but…nice."

I'm tempted to chuckle at this entire situation. Because if I don't laugh, I might cry. What are we doing? Are we about to braid each other's hair and talk about our feelings? I don't think so. I don't want to be in the middle of whatever they may have going on, but at some point, she should also leave me alone. My eyes must still be red from the crying. "Listen, I appreciate you coming here. Even though I wonder why because if I'm honest with you, I think you want Lucas back and I think you don't like me very much. It's a feeling I have."

She purses her lips and nods as if she's thinking and then she tilts her head. The sympathy look is gone from her face, it's more restrained. "I want what's best for him." She pauses and steps towards my couch. Her hand touch the picture Mia drew for me. "And I still want you to know that nothing happened between me and him yesterday." She shrugs and plops on my couch and I'm not sure what to do. Ask her to leave? Offer her coffee or water? "It's not easy, that's all."

My phone rings and I glance at it—half hoping that it's Lucas calling to apologize, but it's my parents. When I don't pick up, they call again. And seeing it's super late in the night in the city, my throat tightens. What if something happened?

"You can take that if you want. I'll wait."

I'd love to ask her to leave but we're in that music video together. And clearly she's trying to do what's best for Lucas. Letting him decide. I pick up the phone. "Hi Mom," I answer and gesture I'm going in the bathroom.

"How are you doing honey?" She asks, her tone worried.

"I'm fine. I'm okay. Busy but good. Why are you calling at this time?"

"I don't know. I couldn't sleep. And then I thought with the time difference I could check up on you. Are you sure you're okay?"

"I'm very sure. I'll figure it out."

She breathes out as if she was relieved to hear my words and after chatting for a few more minutes, I promise to call her back tomorrow and we hang up.

Olivia's still sitting on my couch and she stands up when she sees me. "I really wanted to let you know that nothing happened."

"Why?" I can't help but ask because even if she wants Lucas to make the decision of his own, she still wants him back. Us being mad at each other is actually a good way for her to get what she wants.

"Because he was hurting and I hate seeing him hurt." She glances away and I'm not sure I believe her—maybe it's in the way she said the word 'hurting' like she didn't care if he did hurt or not, but I let it slide. This situation is already as awkward as it can get and me being jealous—because that burning sensation in my chest feels a lot like jealousy—isn't helping.

LOVE IN B MINOR

"Listen, thank you for coming, but I have to get going."

She stands up and her hair floats around her face. Her cherry lips curve into a smile, but it's not a warm smile, it's more a "I've done what I was supposed to do" smile, as if telling me that nothing happened was one more way to prove to Lucas she's changed. And it seems she has and I need to stop thinking about all of this, because the sharp pain in my heart hasn't subsided ever since he slammed the door on our possible real beginning last night.

"I'll see you after our trip," she says with a voice so full of honey that I'm going to get sick from too much sugar just listening to her.

"Bye," I tell her and close the door behind her. I lean against it for a second, my eyes trained to the ceiling. Rehearsals begin in an hour. I need to get moving and I need to get Lucas out of my mind.

At least for now.

***

The rest of the week is grueling. The rehearsals get harder each time and I don't understand how Igor still has his voice after yelling at us for so many hours.

"Steve is doing good. Super busy but good. Lucas, on the other hand, is apparently angry at the world, angry at himself and super sad." Alisha links her arm with mine as we walk outside the studio and into the courtyard for a short break.

"He hasn't called," I reply and even though I try to sound like I don't care, my voice still sounds sad.

"Steve said he and Dimitri want to talk to him. Maybe that will help."

I open my mouth. Then close it. I want to know what's going on with Olivia. He told me it was over, but after her visit to my apartment, I know she's definitely not over him and I'm not sure how I feel about all of this.

Alisha pushes some of the gravel with her foot and then bumps her hip into mine in a sign of understanding. "Steve said Lucas is very professional with Olivia but that nothing is going on. Olivia seems to also not be pushing for anything right now."

LOVE IN B MINOR

Breathing in and out is easier after hearing her words. "I saw my therapist the other day." My new doctor is helping. I was hesitant at first, confiding in someone new, but talking to him has helped alleviate some of my anxieties.

"You told me."

"He asked me to recap some of what happened and then asked me about the particular moment Lucas and I fought."

Alisha pulls out a cigarette and lights it up. "This is the last one." I raise one eyebrow at her and she continues. "And what did you figure out?"

"That he was really on edge that night, that it hasn't been easy for any of us. I'm basically less angry. I still want an explanation but I'm less angry."

Alisha nudges me. "You both need to be willing to fight for each other. It can't be a one-way street."

I repeat her words. She's right. I know she's right. And maybe when Lucas is back, we can sit down and see where we're at.

I also realized that what happened to me in Cape Cod is my story to tell, if I want to tell it and right now I want to share it with Alisha. Because in the past weeks and months, she's becoming a real friend.

I give her the short version since we can't be late for the second part of our rehearsal. When I'm done, I lean back on my heels, waiting for a reaction, any reaction. Worried that she might look at me differently but also more at ease with the fact that this story is part of me, part of who I am, but doesn't define me.

She blinks rapidly as if she's trying not to cry, throws her cigarette in the ashtray and pulls me into a hug.

"I'm sorry," she says with tears in her voice. "I'm sorry you had to go through that." She pauses and leans back with a small smile. "And it's not pity, okay? It's me being your friend and feeling bad you went through such a tough time."

I nod and smile back.

"One minute!" We can overhear Igor yelling from the rehearsing room. He opened one of the small windows and pokes his head out. "You two, come back inside. Now!"

"Yes, sir." We both reply at the same time, and we stroll back inside, I feel more confident.

CHAPTER 47 – LUCAS

The views from our hotel are gorgeous. The mountains in the distance, the colors of the evening in the sky, the lake that's frozen. The animal's tracks making their way from tree to tree. It's peaceful. Benji had always wanted to come here—in Font Romeu, which is close to the Spanish border, because that's where the French national soccer team trained. He thought he could meet them, be like them. He never got to. We were supposed to go on tour the month after he died and he never go to travel here.

LOVE IN B MINOR

The shots for the music video are even more meaningful for me. It's even more meaningful that we do it here. The air is pure and the silence is welcoming after what happened in Paris.

Olivia sits next to me. "We should go skiing tomorrow."

"I don't feel like it. But you should go. I think Grégoire was thinking about it too."

She breathes out in the way she used to when she was annoyed, when she said I didn't pay her enough attention. "You need to have some fun too," she finally says before getting up. "I'm going to bed. I'll see you tomorrow."

"Bye." I keep on staring out of the window. My food—a cheesy potatoes dish—is getting cold, but I don't care. Minutes pass. And I can't get out of my head.

"Man, we've got to talk." Steve and Dimitri stand in front of me, with their arms crossed like they're on a mission

"What?" I didn't intend to bark but I do. It sounds like I'm about to bite.

"You've been in a shitty mood the entire week, and I have it from a good source that you blew up at Jen. She's pissed. She's hurt and she's pissed."

There's a shift in my chest. Hearing her name is a depressing music to my ear. "I don't want to talk about it."

Dimitri pulls a chair and plops himself in front of me, while Steve sits on the bench next to me. Dimitri raises one eyebrow. He usually keeps out of the others' personal lives, so he means business. "You need to think about three things. One, why did you get so upset. Two, what do you want—and I'm not talking professionally, I'm talking personally—and three, how can you get your head out of your ass long enough to see you were most probably wrong?"

My eyes widen, while Steve chuckles. "Well said. I stand with you getting your head out of your ass because again, according to my source—" He pauses and drinks some of my water. "By the way, the source has legs that don't finish and my source is the sweetest and smartest…anyways, my source says that if you knew Jen, you'd know she'd never do that to you."

LOVE IN B MINOR

"But…"

"No buts." Dimitri stands back up. "Think about what I said and then think about ways to make it right. Even if you don't get back together, she doesn't deserve to be treated like shit just because you're insecure."

Steve takes another sip of my water and stands up too. "What he said." And they leave together. This trip definitely helped the band get closer before the release of our new song, before Steve's big debut. I stare outside of the window. The darkness settles on the mountains. And my mind replays for the thousandth time what happened in Jen's apartment. And for the thousandth time, I want to take my words back.

***

How do you say you're sorry to someone?

My reaction was way too strong. And it was way too much based on my past without even giving her the benefit of the doubt. She has every right to be pissed at me, but not talking to her, not hearing her laugh, not joking with her and talking about history, is killing me.

373

As soon as we're back in Paris, I snap a picture of a plaque by the club we were at the first night we met, and I text it to her together with: "I was an asshole, no picture or Parks & Rec quote could save my assholery, but I am so sorry. I have a hard time believing happiness is at reach and trusting people."

She doesn't answer right away. I wave to Karim at the club and in French ask him, "You never called me about that mugger, did everything go okay?"

"Bigger fish was caught." He smiles and opens the door for me. "Where is your lady friend?"

"Hopefully I didn't screw it up completely."

My phone buzzes and I fumble to open the text. "I know. I have issues but I'm working on mine. I think you should work on yours." And maybe she's right. Maybe, I should.

I'll think about it. Can you please come to our club?

Our club? I thought it was Bjorn the Actor's club?

He's not there. Promise. I miss you.

I miss you too.

LOVE IN B MINOR

Let's start over.

No.

No? I gulp my drink as I read her answer. I can see she's typing again.

I don't want to pretend the past weeks didn't happen. A relationship isn't always about songs and it's not always magic. What I want is to move forward...with you. Or at least see you and see if I'm still super mad or only a little bit mad.

I smile at her answer. *When can you get here?*

Give me twenty minutes.

I'll give you all the time in the world. And I add a winking smiley because I know she's going to get my cheesiness. Because in true *Parks & Rec* fashion, she's the April to my Andy.

That would be a long time to sit in that club. I'm pretty sure they close at 5 a.m.

This time my chuckle is louder. I can't wait to see her, to wrap my arms around her. To be with her. Because I trust her, because I want to move forward.

She arrives right on time. "You're much cuter than Bjorn the Actor—you should have totally bought me a drink that night."

"I baked you cookies."

She bites the side of her lower lip, and I'm not sure she realizes it but my gaze focuses on her mouth.

"They were delicious cookies," she replies. And then clears her throat. "How were the mountains?"

"They were inspirational. I talked a lot with Dimitri and Steve. And then I thought a lot. I realized I'm putting my past on you, and I don't want to do that."

"I do the same. I mean, I think you can't escape your past. You can't just forget about it, but I do believe that you rushed to conclusions. I thought you knew me, and you thinking that I'd do anything to hurt you… That was painful."

"I think it was because of seeing Olivia again and remembering all those times she basically used me to move forward. And then remembering all those rumors about her and Benji. It was tough and I'm so sorry I ended up projecting on you. It wasn't fair."

LOVE IN B MINOR

"Thank you. For saying that. I am not taking back what I said about the show. If you don't want to do it, it's your decision and I would need to accept it, but it's important to me, because it's important to the company and to the people I dance with."

I link my fingers with hers, revealing in the feel of her skin against mine, anticipating what might be. And a side of my mouth curves up into a small smile before I kiss each of her knuckles. "I know. And I respect that. And I'll do it."

"Really? Not because you want to get in my pants, right?"

I lean forward until we almost touch. I can feel her body slightly move forward too, like it cannot wait to melt into mine. "That's just an added bonus." And our breaths mix, our lips meet, I'm the one melting in her arms.

CHAPTER 48 – JEN

The way back to my apartment is all laughter and serious conversations and jokes and deep thoughts. It's everything. Our hips keep on bumping against one another as if we were trying to find additional ways to connect.

My body hums in harmony with his voice. Those stupid rules we tried to follow were only the walls we tried so hard to erect around ourselves. So what if more stories will come out? So what if people are going to know I made mistakes? Grégoire has decided the best moment to share my story would be the day the video is released. He's planning interviews based on the email I got earlier from him. So what if they think I'm the troublemaker between Lucas and Olivia? I understand now that their relationship was over even before Benji passed away. They grew apart. She's right about one thing: the pictures and the lies were not the reason Lucas left her, it was that they took separate paths.

We turn into my street and into my building. "Race you to the top," I say, laughing and climbing stairs as quickly as possible, but I'm not fast enough and Lucas catches me by the waist.

"I'm not letting you go," he whispers in my ear, and his strong arm around me sends waves of heat throughout my body. A delicious tingle runs down my spine.

"Are you going to bake me cookies?" My voice is husky and full of want. Before I might have tried to turn it down, but no longer. I can no longer deny myself.

"Maybe…do you even have the right utensils?"

ELODIE NOWODAZKIJ

"Hey…" I protest but then laugh with him, because he's right, I probably don't.

My fingers shake from anticipation but I manage to unlock my front door. And as soon as we're inside, his mouth is on mine, taking and giving. And my back is against the door. I pepper kisses on his neck and his smell—a mix of cologne and Paris and the now and the future—envelops me. I shrug out of my coat and my cardigan, and his fingers find the hem of my shirt and he slowly, very slowly raises it, teasing me and tempting me. Touching my skin that's on fire.

"Come on." I breathe out and he finally takes my shirt off; I do the same with his and his skin is against mine. His skin is warm and paler than mine. My fingers trail up and down his muscular torso and my lips follow the same path. He leans back and watches me and his gaze on me is an additional turn-on—it makes me feel wanted and beautiful.

"I want you so much," he tells me before kissing me again. And then his hands are everywhere. And it's even better than what I remember. He pulls me up and my legs wrap around his waist, he walks us to my bed and at first he takes his time and I take mine. We explore each other's bodies but then, it's like we can no longer wait. And when we're finally one, I close my eyes.

***

The next morning is not awkward. It's fun and playful and sexy.

"Are you sure you have to go?" he asks, pulling me back to him.

"I do have to go. Grégoire sent me another email about meeting him for coffee to discuss the interviews he has in mind for my big reveal." Lucas' body is warm and comfy.

"I'm sorry you have to do that," he says, with one finger trailing down my naked arm, giving me the most pleasurable goosebumps.

"I'm not. I think it might be good to talk about it. Not only for me, but for others, you know. Like, I started taking drugs when I was dancing. And clearly I wasn't the only one. And then this need to fit it. This fear of saying 'no' back then—I'm sure I'm not the only one." I kiss his cheek, because if I kiss him the way I want to, I'll never leave. "My therapist said that if I felt strong enough to do it, and if I felt like I could help people, it might be good for me too."

"You're amazing." His eyes hold so much awe and so much tenderness in them that I want to bottle the feeling I have and keep it forever.

"Thank you. You too. Now let me go, otherwise Grégoire is going to yell and you know it's not good for his health." I stand up. "The door will lock itself behind you. I'll see you at the shooting later today?"

"Are you ready for the choreography?"

"According to Igor, I'm as ready as I will be."

And I head out with his laughter resonating in my mind and in my heart. Grégoire wants to meet in a place on the outskirts of Paris I'm not very familiar with yet, so I use my phone for direction. One train ride later I should be close by. At least it's not dark outside because this place seems shady. I turn into a street where the windows of the houses are broken. Some guy whistles as I walk by and I ignore him, which earns me a call of "Bitch," and even the fact it's said in French doesn't make it less insulting I'm about to text Grégoire when I hear her.

Mia. My sister. It's her voice. What the hell?

"Jen! Jen, come here!" I'm not going crazy. I'm not going crazy. I'm not crazy. I keep on repeating those words as I step in the direction of her voice.

There are steps behind me. I look back but I don't see anyone. Mia's voice is closer. My heart thumps faster and faster. "Time to die, Jen," Mia's voice whispers.

I want to scream, but a hand shoves a tissue in my mouth and something on my nose.

And my steps become uncoordinated.

And my breathing shallows, and my hands clamp up and the world turns.

And then, nothing.

CHAPTER 49 – LUCAS

Everything was going too well. I should have known better.

Alisha's call has me worried, like a feeling running deep that something is wrong. "Alisha, calm down. What do you mean she didn't come to the rehearsal? She's never missed a rehearsal. Igor told me that once she came to rehearse at four in the morning before everyone. She was burning hot and didn't want to infect anybody, but still wanted to rehearse. And I thought you guys didn't have any rehearsals today, we're supposed to shoot in an hour."

LOVE IN B MINOR

"Audrey texted us that Igor wanted one extra rehearsal today. It was supposed to be from ten this morning to twelve, so then she still had enough time to meet you guys at two. But she didn't come."

"She had a meeting with Grégoire this morning. She was meeting him for breakfast. Let me call him. Maybe they're still together."

"Call me back, okay?"

I walk to Jen's kitchen. I didn't find anything to bake cookies, but I thought I'd order some food online and have them delivered so I could surprise her with warm cookies when she got back. Even though her apartment is not much decorated, she can be seen in the tulips standing in a vase by her small window.

I dial Grégoire's work number but he doesn't pick up, so I try his personal cell. "You're up early," he says and he almost sounds happy to hear my voice.

"Is Jen still with you?" I ask.

"Why would Jen be with me?" His voice is genuinely confused and a chill runs down my spine.

"Because you guys were having breakfast to discuss opportunities for her talking about her episode with drugs."

"Hmmm, we do need to talk about it, but I wasn't going to meet her this morning. I thought I'd bring it up when we all meet this afternoon."

"Where is your work phone? Why didn't you pick up?"

"I lost it last night."

This time, the chills running down my spine turn icy cold. "I have to call you back."

***

After calling the police, and mentioning the fact that someone must have impersonated Grégoire, I got Alisha up to speed. The police got her old cell phone from Grégoire and mentioned due to the amount of death threats she received, they would take this seriously. They questioned Grégoire for several hours, since apparently his work phone was also used to make death threats to Jen. He denies it and I can't believe it either.

LOVE IN B MINOR

The band met up at Steve's apartment since he's the closest to the police station. Alisha's already there. It actually looks like she's been spending a few days there.

We talk in circles that don't bring any answers, and my patience is running thin.

"Where could she be? She doesn't know anyone else in Paris!" My voice rises and the rest of the group turns my way. Olivia tilts her head to the side and then stands up to sit by me. She's not crowding me but simply whispers.

"I'm sure everything is going to be okay. They'll find her."

I want to scream. I want to break everything. The police asked if maybe she had talked about leaving, about feeling too much pressure. She didn't. And she wouldn't disappear like this knowing what it would do to her friends, to me, to her parents. Her show is in two weeks, and the video should release next week. The final days of shooting were this week. Her parents got tickets to come visit her. "Oh wait, didn't she mention that her mom had a friend in Paris, a designer?"

Alisha shakes slightly and Steve wraps an arm around her. "I can't recall her name and she went there once for dinner, but that's it."

Dimitri paces around the room. "Still, why don't you see with her parents who that friend is?"

Alisha whimpers but then squares her shoulder like having something to do to help, anything, is giving her a purpose. "I'll get her parents' phone number from Igor, but I'm worried, Lucas. I'm really worried."

She stands up and we hug. Steve follows her. "I'll walk Alisha to the door downstairs, I'll be right back."

I bury my head in my hands. My heart hammers loudly. It resonates everywhere like a bad song. It can't be the same. It won't be the same.

The phone call from Olivia freaking out about Benji's whereabouts, saying he was sad and depressed. The search. The body at the rave. His dead body.

I can't lose her. I can't lose her too.

CHAPTER 50 - JEN

My limbs are freezing. It's cold. So cold in this room. Like there hasn't been any heating in months. The musty smell infiltrates everything. The mask on my face doesn't move, and all I can distinguish through it is that there are lights in another room. The door must be open—I could try to wobble on my feet and then run.

"Jen. Jen, I love you!" Mia's voice stops me, freezes me. "Jen!" I want to throw my hands on my ears, but they're tight behind my back. "I'm dead now, I'm dead." She sings songs now and I want to yell, I want to tell whoever is doing this to stop, to leave my sister alone.

The lump in my throat tightens. My mind is fuzzy and foggy. Not sure if it's because of the chloroform or because of the fact I haven't eaten anything in…how long have I been here?

I was going to meet Grégoire. I was going to meet Grégoire to talk about my interviews. I only stepped into that side street because I heard Mia's voice. Mia. Oh my God, what's going on?

A door screeches open. My heart beats faster. It gallops in my chest.

The steps etch closer.

"Don't worry, not much more time…"

CHAPTER 51 - LUCAS

The night passed by way too slowly. Jen has disappeared for almost twenty-four hours, and the police are still investigating.

For once, I'm grateful for everyone following my whereabouts. It helps the police clear me quickly and someone recalls seeing Jen stepping into an RER that goes toward the north of Paris. She was smiling. She didn't seem distraught. I don't get it.

Jen's parents took a redeye to Paris and are arriving at Charles de Gaulle in less than an hour, and we have nothing. Nothing more. "Did you tell them they could stay with me? Your dad is trying to come back from his explorations in Greece as soon as possible. He's sorry he can't be there." Mom looks like she hasn't slept since I called her with the news. She's never met Jen, but she said every single time I talked about her, I sounded happy. Genuinely happy.

"I did tell them," I reply with a quick hug. "I also sent a driver to pick them up and bring them to the station."

"I can't even imagine." Mom hugs me again, this time tighter, as if she doesn't want to let me go. "I don't want to imagine." She kisses my cheek and then nods. "Bonjour, Olivia." She smiles, and for once it's not one of those you-broke-my-son's-heart smiles, so there's progress.

But there's no progress on the investigation. They got her phone calls but are trying to access her text messages.

Olivia sits next to me. "Any news?"

"Nothing."

LOVE IN B MINOR

She stares straight ahead. "Her parents. I don't know how they're going to feel." She stands back up. "I have to do something, anything. I'll get more pictures on social media and might see if we can set up a phone center. To get tips or anything that can help."

I squeeze her hand. "Thank you so much."

"Of course! I'm so sorry." She stands up and grabs her phone, before heading out.

"Olivia has been useful," Mom says with a snide tone, and then she shakes her head. "I should be quiet, I'm sorry."

Inspector Roger enters the room. "Jen's parents are here. We'll talk to them first, but maybe you'd like to bring them to their hotel afterwards. They look…" His face is drawn and pale as if even though he sees this type of shit every day, he's not used to it, as if he never wants to get used to it. "They look like they will need support."

And he was right.

Jen's mom is crying while her father holds on to his wife like she's the only one who makes sense.

When we meet them in the hallway of the station, Jen's mom tries to stop her tears.

"She sounded happy. She sounded like she wasn't afraid to be herself…Jen used to close up so easily, to put up a front. I know she's learned it from me…when Mia got sick, I couldn't deal." She sniffles, and Mom stands up and opens her arms.

"We're doing everything we can," she whispers in her ear while Jen's father stares at me with wide eyes.

"We can't lose her too." His voice breaks. This big man who looks like he could be the son of Muhammad Ali and Klitschko is about to cry. He pulls out a picture from his pocket. "That's our Jen, right there. When she wasn't dancing, she was taking pictures, or finding ways to look at the events unfolding in front of her in a different way. We have to find her."

"We will."

The police come back with frowns on their faces. "We need to talk to you again, quickly."

LOVE IN B MINOR

"Can't you say it right here?" Jen's dad sounds angry now and then he glances down. "I'm sorry, it's not about you, it's just…my baby girl."

"We'll talk to all of you, but in the room on the right—let's not do this in the middle of the station."

And we follow him, Mom holding Jen's mom's hand and me walking side by side with her father.

"We brought the dog to Jen's apartment and he found something."

"What?"

"Three grams of heroin behind the drawing I assume her sister made for her."

Jen's mom stands up. "No, no, no, no, no." She sits back down and her husband pulls her to him. "That can't be. She hasn't touched drugs since that one summer years ago, it cannot be." She turns me. "You believe me, right? She'd never do that to her sister. She'd never do it to herself. She worked so hard on herself, she worked so hard for everything."

"I know." And I do. It doesn't make any sense. Nothing makes sense.

***

The rest of the day is a blur. Jen's parents decide to stay in a hotel but accept Mom's invitation to come over for dinner. They're both tired and devastated and they clutch one another.

"Jen was always amazing at ballet, and maybe I pushed her too hard." Her mom has tears in her voice. "But then I thought if I don't push her, she might resent me later. She might resent me for not nurturing her talent."

"She loves dancing." I push my food around my plate, unable to eat anything. "She told me how much she loves dancing. She said that dancing helps her, has helped her—even when it was hard, even when people yelled at her, she loves it."

"She does, right?" Her mom looks at me with gratitude in her eyes and then, she pulls her hair up and my breath catches in my throat. I have to glance away before I make Jen's mom uncomfortable for staring. They have the same way of dealing with stress. "When she steps on stage, she's transformed, she's in the moment, she forgets everything that's not dancing." She sniffles and Mom covers her hand with hers.

LOVE IN B MINOR

There's a kinship between the two of them. Maybe it's because when we lost Benji, Mom felt like she lost another son. Or maybe because Mom sees how much I'm hurting.

"Are you sure you don't want to stay with us? My husband will be back tomorrow. He's flying back from an archeology trip in Greece and with the strikes, he couldn't make it back yet."

Jen's parents shake their heads. "We took a hotel right next to the police station. We want to be there in a heartbeat if they call."

"I understand," Mom replies and then it's time to leave, time to go back to my empty apartment, because I can't stay home either. I want to be in the city, I want to be close by if something does come up. When they find her.

Because they will find her.

CHAPTER 52 - JEN

No one will ever find me. That voice. It can't be Mia. They must use some sort of system to alter their voice. I force myself to breathe steadily through my nose. Whoever holds me captive is now gone. And if they're acting alone, then maybe I have a window of opportunity. One thing about being a ballerina is that I am not only flexible but I'm also strong, stronger than I look. I rock from side to side, trying to find some place to cut my ties.

There's nothing.

LOVE IN B MINOR

Nothing at all.

But I'll keep trying.

CHAPTER 53 – LUCAS

My mind can't stop running in circles, thinking about possibilities and how the police asked if I had received any threats. I can't remember anything. My doorbell rings and I rush to answer, hoping against all hope that it's Jen—simply swinging back into our lives like nothing has happened.

"It's me," Olivia says. "I thought you might want some company."

I don't.

I really don't. But I also don't want to send her back on her way without at least thanking her for everything she's been doing. She's been such a rock. So much stronger than I thought she could be. And for the second time in a short while, I can picture us actually being friends. I want her to be happy.

"Thanks. Come on up." I buzz her in.

"I brought you a kebab—I'm pretty sure you haven't eaten anything today, and it's from your favorite place." My stomach growls at the smell. I haven't eaten my dinner and my lunch was made of two bites of my Panini.

"You know me," I tell her with a small smile, a smile that's probably a shadow of the last real one I had with Jen. In her apartment. Watching *Parks & Rec.* In her bed. After making love. My throat tightens and Olivia takes my hand in hers. It's comforting. "I am really grateful for everything you've done." My voice is gruff, but she tilts her head to the side.

"Let me find something on TV, and why don't you come and sit on the couch to eat your kebab. You have to relax. You have to sleep. You have to be one hundred percent there if you want to help find Jen."

She's right. I know she's right. So I let myself be guided to the couch, and she puts on France 2 on the TV, where the first movie of the evening is about to start. It's an older movie, a funny one about a group of people finding themselves on holiday together. I bite into the kebab and even though it's hard to eat, even though I don't feel like having the company, I can't deny this is exactly what I needed.

Olivia nestles next to me, tucking her feet under herself like she used to do, trailing her fingers down my arm like she used to do, and then leaning against my shoulder once I'm done eating like she used to do.

Except I'm not time traveling. This is not the reincarnation of our past relationship and even though I'm grateful for everything she's done, I can't blur the lines.

I slide a bit to the right, carefully to not hurt her feelings.

She doesn't get the memo and slides back next to me. "This feels good, doesn't it?"

"What?" Playing dumb might be the best solution right now because I don't have the strength to face whatever she's talking about. She has to know this isn't going to work. Shit, I'm worried about another woman while she's trying to rekindle our long gone past.

"Us." She rises and her lips touch my neck, my cheek.

I breathe out and stand up, putting more distance between us, physically and figuratively. "There is no us," I say as gently as possible. I've come a long way in the past month to finally put that "us" behind me, where it belongs. I've forgiven her and accepted that we were simply not meant to be, that she didn't try to hurt me, that she cared.

"Of course there is," she whispers and slowly stands up. She licks her lips and the way she moves reminds me of other times. Of that past I no longer want to live in.

"There's not, Olivia. You know there's not."

And when she throws her arms around me, I push her back. She plops back down on the couch. Confusion etches across her face in the way her eyes widen, in the way her mouth gapes.

"We're over," I explain and I'm taken aback by the way she acted. After pretending to be so worried about Jen. "No matter what, we're over."

"It's that little bitch, isn't it?"

And this time when she stands up, confusion has been replaced with hatred and anger and I'm not sure what's going on. "You think she loves you? You think she even fucking cares about you?" Olivia paces around me. "Do you have any idea of how much I've done for you?"

And my breathing stops for a second. Because this can't be true. This can't be. She's Olivia—she's my first love, the one who laughed with me and cried with me for years, the one who was there for me and Benji.

"I get it, you're scared. You're scared about your love for me. You're scared of what people would think." She rambles and then stops and stares at me. "Benji couldn't get between us; I won't let her get between us either."

"Benji?" Blood freezes in my veins, everything stops and I need to sit down. "What the fuck are you talking about?"

LOVE IN B MINOR

"Oh come on, don't tell me you really believed me when I told you Benji and I had nothing going on. I had to keep myself busy while you were becoming famous. Benji was there." There's no emotion in her voice. There's no emotion whatsoever. This can't be Olivia, there must be a mistake.

But then my brain processes what she just said. "You killed Benji."

"I gave him what he needed. He was hooked. He was trying to stop but he didn't have it in him. He was wasting space and perfectly good air. How do you think I got those pictures I somehow leaked to the press using a fake profile? When you hugged me and held me tight, it made it all okay."

"Jen? Where is Jen?"

"You think I'm going to tell you. After you rejected me. Again." There's a sardonic light in her eyes, like she doesn't believe I've been such an idiot. But I haven't seen it, any of it. "My nannies always wondered what was wrong with me, but I could hide it from my parents. They didn't care enough."

"What do you mean?"

She laughs and it's actually a laugh I've heard before, it's a laugh that I thought meant she was having a good time, and maybe she is. "When my little brother died accidentally." She air quotes "accidentally" and I stare at her, horrified. "What? He was way too loud and taking too much attention. It was painless for him. And Mom did shake him twice before I took care of him. Clearly, she didn't do any damage, but it was enough to plant a seed of doubt in her mind. And she didn't get punished since no one could prove anything."

I don't have any words. I don't know what to say. I don't know how to deal with the way my bones chill.

She continues as if she told me it was raining outside, not that she killed her own brother. "Anyways, Nanny Number Three really wondered about me. She wondered about some of my reactions. According to her, I didn't cry enough, I didn't show enough emotions. I learned a lot from her really on how to get better at pretending. But, she cared too much, really. She wondered so much I had to let her go."

"What do you mean?"

LOVE IN B MINOR

"It was so easy; making sure my brother stopped stealing all the attention away from me didn't faze me. He was the first person I killed and I didn't feel anything. So doing it a second time with the nanny? It wasn't hard. No remorse, none of this bullshit that always brings people down."

I'm going to get sick. I wobble on my feet, holding myself to the counter of the kitchen. "What did you do?"

"I was thirteen. She convinced my parents I needed to see someone, and they let her take me to a therapist. They let her sit on my appointment. I didn't care. I didn't give a shit. I could weasel my way out of things." She smiles, and this time it's her signature Olivia smile—sweet and I thought genuine, but her words chill me to the bone. "He said, and I quote, that I had psychopath tendencies with a full narcissist complex. He said I needed help…" She giggles. "On our way back, we were waiting for our train in La République metro station and some pickpocket was running around. People were scrambling and I used that opportunity."

"What?"

"I pushed her in front of the metro…and went home by myself, telling my parents that the nanny had said she quit."

I'm going to throw up. I'm going to scream and throw up, but I need to know where Jen is. I need to know if she's still alive.

"That was ballsy."

"Right? They never suspected a thing. I was holding her purse for her, pretending to look for my phone, which I told her I had left in there. So, she had no ID card. I knew the cameras they had at the time didn't record the entire platform. The pickpocket was arrested and they never could identify her. It was brilliant."

"How about Benji?"

"Benji and I had one night together. I seduced him while he was drunk and I knew he'd been crushing on me for years, so it wasn't too hard to play the Damsel in Distress, crying over your absences and how I didn't feel loved anymore. Oh, he made me feel love, all right." She doesn't see how disgusted I am by her words, how frightened they make me. "Then, he got too hung up on me. He wanted to stop taking drugs, and I could not let that happen. He needed to go, he needed to go before he told you what happened. He was feeling so bad, so guilty." She chuckles, shaking her head like it's the stupidest thing she's ever heard. "Guilt is such a useless feeling to have. Aren't you supposed to live your life without regrets? Isn't that better than to live with remorse? Well, I don't regret sleeping with Benji. He wasn't too shitty, and I have no remorse in giving him his fatal dose."

"Please tell me you didn't." My throat closes up and my eyes dart to the alarm system I have in this place. The panic button Mom had me install after Benji's death, after the fans got angry at the band splitting up, is right under the counter where Olivia sits. She doesn't know it's here, she can't know it's here. I step forward. "Please tell me you didn't kill him."

"Well theoretically speaking, the heroin killed him. Like the heroin is going to kill that little Jen of yours."

"You won't be able to get away with it." One more step...I only need one more step to reach the counter.

She glances down and then back up. Her eyes bore into mine. "I thought you and I had something special. Benji was a distraction, I wanted you. I still want you. You were always the one I was supposed to be with. Remember Shawna?"

I nod. She still holds my eyes and I can't move. I feel like my movements would be too revealing and she would know exactly what I'm up to. "I remember Shawna." Shawna was a girl I had a crush on the year I met Olivia. She was bubbly and cute and had the biggest smile. I asked her on a date and she said yes. I wanted to kiss her so badly and I was about to take the plunge, when I found a note she wrote to another guy telling him how much she loved him and wanted to be with him. She denied it but it was her notebook. I dumped her and moved on. It was hard at first, but Olivia and I started seeing each other and I forgot everyone who wasn't her.

LOVE IN B MINOR

"You wrote that letter." The melody of my life is turning out to be much different than the one I thought I composed for it.

"Of course I did. Shawna wasn't meant for you. I was. When you dumped me, I was devastated. For the first time in my life I wasn't getting what I wanted. And what I wanted was you. Benji was dead. I had tried that solo career when you took that break from music, and then you dump me?"

She sighs and takes her eyes off of me. It's now or never. I step forward. But she moves too, faster than me. "If I were you, I'd forget about pressing that alarm."

I must look as dumbfounded as I feel, because she continues. "I've got a tiny camera in the bookshelves over there—I put it in when I came to the apartment to gather my stuff. Your mom was right to ask you to put an alarm. You never know what can happen, where danger lurks."

"You don't have to do that. We can be together."

"You think I'm an idiot. The last plea before you save yourself and your loved one? I found a pretty good way to get rid of her, very symbolic too." She tilts her heard. "Grand-mère Julie would appreciate the romanticism in all that."

And then it hits me. "Please tell me you had nothing to do with her heart attack!"

"You think I go visit the old woman every single day? Of course I pushed her from her bed. It was so easy. There was no one in the hallway and she was sleeping, I simply gave her a shove. I didn't think she would get a heart attack." She plays with her hair like we're discussing in which restaurant we should eat dinner, or what song we should be singing next, not her killing people. She smiles fondly at me and I swallow the insults and questions I want to throw at her. She chuckles. "You're so gullible, you believe everything I said despite everything that's happened between us." She pauses. "Maybe I should bring you to Jen. Maybe you should die together there—it could be cathartic for you. Step back so you don't inadvertently press that alarm button." I do as she says. And then she shuffles in the purse. "Where is it? Oh, here. You have to love my mom for not locking her gun." She pulls out a small handgun.

Her phone rings and she frowns. "Benji's number? That doesn't make any sense."

I rush forward, and shove her backwards with all my strength. "What are you doing?" The gun goes off and there's a sharp burning pain in my shoulder, but the adrenaline runs through me and I hold her down. "Where is Jen?"

And for a split second when she simply grins my way—a grin I used to love and now have come to fear—I'm tempted to simply squeeze her neck, to stop her from grinning. But I let go of her.

"Police!" someone screams from outside and a swat team storms into my apartment. The detective in charge of Jen's disappearance attempts to move me out of the way. "We got this," he tells me, but his words don't reassure me.

"She's got Jen." My voice is raspy but still strong and the detective nods.

"I'm not going to fucking go to jail," Olivia screams and lunches forward for her gun, but the detective kicks it away and a policewoman grabs her. "It's all their fault! They should have known better!" Her screams get louder and louder but the police handcuff her and carry her out—unfazed by the litany of obscenities she's now yelling.

"Are you okay?" the detective asks me and no, no I'm not okay. My shoulder will be fine, but my entire mind can't wrap itself around the fact that Olivia was responsible. Responsible for all of this. Responsible for so many deaths. Responsible for so many tears.

I was in love with her. I was in love with a monster. But I don't want to think about that now. I don't want to think about anything but saving Jen. When Olivia said something about Grand-mère Julie and my happy memories, I remembered we kept Benji's house. We didn't sell it because I told them I wasn't ready to let go of my happy memories.

LOVE IN B MINOR

"Jen. She has to be in Benji's house, it's an old house at the outskirts of Paris. It's almost falling apart now."

"We'll send someone there. And you need to go to the hospital. You've been shot."

CHAPTER 54 – JEN

When loud steps can be heard through the house, I'm almost ready to fight. I manage to roll by some broken glass from a window and while I cut myself and am probably bleeding profusely, my hands and feet are now free.

I tried to find a way to kick the door open, but it was impossible.

And even if my head turns and even if I feel like my brain is surrounded by cotton and even though my heart is beating way too fast, I know it's my last chance.

LOVE IN B MINOR

"Police!" one person screams, but it could be the same trick used before. Something to change the voice.

"I don't believe you." There are tears in my eyes.

But then several people talk at once and I slide to the floor. I feel myself being carried and put in an ambulance where Mom and Dad hold my hands. For a second, I see Mia with them and she's smiling and she's telling me that everything is going to be okay.

***

At the hospital, they stitch me back up and I have to stay on observation for an entire week. My parents almost never leave my side. Olivia is pleading guilty. When she came to visit me after I had found her at Lucas', she put a camera in my kitchen, and the police found it in their second swipe of the apartment. It was linked to her cell phone.

She managed to lure me by using Mia's voice. The hospital had done a short video asking for volunteers, and Mia was in that video—she used her voice sample there to create the illusion of her voice.

417

They still had Benji's phone in the chain of custody, so they used that to distract her while they rushed into Lucas' apartment. I can't even start thinking about what would have happened if they hadn't found me, if they didn't find this camera inside my apartment.

"Can I come in?" Lucas enters one evening, way past visiting hours. His arm in a sling but a bright smile on his face. And my heart thuds faster and faster. I wonder if it's always going to be like this, if my body and heart are always going to react like this when I see him. And even though I know from my parents that staying together is sometimes hard, they also showed me that most of the time, it makes them stronger.

"Sure thing. How is your arm?"

"It still hurts but we're both alive, so I can't seem to be too mad about my stupid arm. I'll be able to play piano again next month, they said."

"That's good. I miss you playing the piano."

"I want to do things to you on the piano." He sits by me and when our arms brush, I feel it. The connection. The anticipation. It's there.

LOVE IN B MINOR

"Is that a promise?" I whisper and he wraps his good arm around me.

"It's a promise."

And his lips find mine. It's a quick kiss. But I still smile. It's the smile reserved only for him—it's playful and flirty and full of memories already. Happy memories. We keep the sad ones close to us, but we talk about it with other people too. With professionals. Because Lucas has to come to terms with the fact that he loved someone who never showed and still doesn't show any empathy. And I know I can't be the one guiding him through all of that. Grégoire is making this into a big special in both a teen magazine and on TV. He's still not very relaxed and he still yells a lot, but at least he's leaving us in peace, and seeing Olivia in jail seem to have taken him down a notch. Apparently, she threatened to take legal action against him if he didn't try to bring her back into the band. She said she could prove he knew who Benji's dealer was. Which she couldn't, but she's a good bluffer.

I bite the inside of my cheek. I turn to him to kiss him again but this time, he teases me. The kiss deepens and I moan in his mouth. And it's only when he grunts because of his arm that I pull back. This is only our beginning—we'll have so many more kisses in the future.

"Will you bake me cookies?"

"Anytime you want."

EPILOGUE – One month later – JEN

The wounds have healed. The physical wounds have healed and the emotional ones are doing much better both for me and Lucas. Grégoire decided to scrap the original plan for the music video for the song about Benji. Instead, they only used the band playing with pictures of Benji growing up, with his grandmother who I now go see with Lucas, with his guitar… Even though I've never met him, it feels like I know him. The news about Olivia has been replaced with other news. Other people. Other tragedies. Olivia apparently has a fan club of men and women writing to her. She's become another type of celebrity, has found another group of admirers.

It sickens me but I try to not think too much about it.

I close my eyes, relishing the wooden smell of the theater where we're performing. The chatter of the other dancers is subdued. We got a standing ovation for our performance of *Giselle*. "Are you ready?" Alisha asks me. She's still wearing her costume from *Giselle*—the show we just put on. Igor agreed to postpone it so I could dance in it.

"As ready as I'll ever be," I reply, hugging her.

My parents are in the audience. And Lucas' parents are in the audience. And the rest of the band. It's the first time we're performing this. The first time anyone except Igor and Grégoire—who wanted to make sure we weren't presenting something unprofessional—sees it.

The first note of the piano calls my name and I step on stage. And I only see him. Lucas at the piano playing our song. Not the one which is on its way to the top of the charts, but another. A melancholic melody, a sad melody at the beginning, but a melody full of hope and tenderness. Of passion and love.

He grins the grin I love. The one that tells me everything I need to know, the one that melts my heart. And I dance to our song "Love in B Minor".

And after the last pirouette, after the last note, after the last word is sung, Lucas stands up, opens his arms and I rush into his embrace, while the audience stands up and claps.

"I love you," Lucas whisper in my ears, and the tingles spreading down my spine are dancing to the same melody as the butterflies in my stomach.

"I love you too."

And I melt into his arms. Forgetting the rest of the world.

In true *Parks & Rec* fashion, which we've been re-watching during our rare spare time, he's the Andy to my April.

THE END

Little note to my readers

Dear Reader,

Thank you SO MUCH for reading LOVE IN B MINOR! I know you have the choice between a lot lot loooot of books and I'm grateful you took a chance on mine.

Hope you enjoyed getting to know Jen & Lucas!

Would you like to read some **bonus scenes**? Leave a review on the e-vendor of your choice for this book and you will receive the **following extra content:**

- An epilogue from Lucas' point of view

- And the scene of Lucas baking cookies from Jen's point of view.

After you leave a review email the link to brokendreamsseries@gmail.com and I will personally send you the bonus content.

If you want regular updates about my writing, the chance to participate in monthly giveaways and more, you can sign up for my newsletter here.

And, if you're interested in reading exclusive excerpts, a place to hang out and talk books, writing, the musicians who inspired Lucas...don't hesitate to join Elodie's Cozy Nook on Facebook

ELODIE NOWODAZKIJ

Other books by the author

One Dream Only

One Two Three

A Summer Like No Other

Always Second Best

Acknowledgements

I'm grateful. I'm happy. I'm lucky. Writing isn't easy. Writing is hard. Writing can be so painful. But writing, while driving me crazy sometimes, also keeps me sane in a lot of ways. And even though I would write even if I had only a few minutes a day like I used to, I can dedicate much more time now thanks to my husband. And you have no idea how much he's done while I was finishing up this book. Thank you for being you, Alex. I love you. And nope, I don't think I'll ever stop using your arms in my novels, I do love them too. (Don't blush). The Two Ps, Plato the Dog and Peter The Cat have helped me too by forcing me to take breaks when I needed it and for being extra cuddly when I needed it too.

This book is the result of many months of search and doubts. And it wouldn't be there without the help of my wonderful and talented critique partners. Thank you Riley Edgewood, Katy Upperman and Alison Miller for keeping me in check and for pushing me and for supporting me. You ladies rock. And as always our annual writing's retreat helped me a whole lot! Thanks also to Cambria and Cristin for your insight and for helping me with that s-alliteration…

And thank you to my copy editor Stephanie Parent ☺, who helps make my words shine.

Tracey gave me puppies on Twitter to motivate me. And all the members of my cozy nook have been extremely supportive and I love hanging out there and I'm grateful for them too.

LOVE IN B MINOR

Thank you to my family. I don't see you as often as I want but I know you're there. And I hope you know I'm there too.

Thank you to my friends, near and far. Your support means the world. And thank you for understanding when I'm holed up in my house, not able to move, not able to do anything except write.

And thank you to everyone reading this little book. It means the world.

About the author

Elodie Nowodazkij was raised in a tiny village in France, where she could always be found a book in hand. At nineteen, she moved to the US, where she learned she'd never lose her French accent. Now she lives in Maryland with her husband, their dog and their cat.

She's also a serial smiley user.

Visit Elodie online at:
www.elodienowodazkij.com
www.facebook.com/elodienowodazkij
twitter.com/ENowodazkij